LYTHAM

ENOUGH BLUE SKY

ENOUGH BLUE SKY

by

ELIZABETH NORTH

LONDON
VICTOR GOLLANCZ LTD
1977

01810742

© Elizabeth North 1977

ISBN 0 575 02251 5

97710320

PRINTED IN GREAT BRITAIN BY
NORTHUMBERLAND PRESS LIMITED
GATESHEAD

To my mother, who got us there.

There's enough blue sky to make a pair of sailor's trousers, so you can go out to play now.

A Nanny saying.

ONE

His Britannic Majesty's Principal Secretary of State for
Foreign Affairs requests and requires in the Name of His
Majesty, all those whom it may concern, to allow the
bearer to pass freely without let or hindrance, and to afford
the bearer such assistance and protection as may be
necessary.

THERE WAS A long walk between the train and the customs
shed, this walk being along the platform in grey December
air which was sharpened by the sea, the port smell and that
extra reflected light which you get by the sea whatever time
of year. Over the low corrugated-iron roof of the customs
shed June saw the funnels of the channel ferries and the seagulls flying, and she strode in her polished brown brogues,
with her new shoulder bag swinging on her right shoulder and
her camel hair coat over her left arm. Her coat-and-skirt,
which she never called a suit or costume, were navy blue
Harris tweed with a box-pleat skirt; her hat was a grey tweed
imitation of a sailor hat, worn off the face with the front
of her hair showing. She strode, the first passenger off the
train, and outstripped those who had started with her along
the platform. She walked fast like she walked across flat fields
at home with dogs and children some way behind.

The children and not the dogs were waiting by the guard's
van for a porter.

On her passport she is June Mary Franklin, born 1901,
height five foot eight, brown hair, blue eyes and no distin-
guishing features. No passport gives the weight of its bearer,
but June could weigh anything between nine-and-a-half and
ten stone and has kept her weight remarkably consistent over

the years of and since the bearing of the children whose names are on her passport:

Prudence June Franklin.	Date of Birth: 1st June 1924.
Alexander Dawson Franklin.	„ „ „: 3rd July 1926.
April Constance Franklin.	„ „ „: 5th April 1930.
Rosalind Jane Franklin.	„ „ „: 7th August 1932.

She aimed to give every one of them birthdays in the summer because her own was in June, and children should have summer treats, strawberries or raspberries with ice cream on birthdays, and be taken to their father's ship if it is in an English port on the south coast, and be lifted up by ratings and petty officers from the Admiral's barge. The plan about a summer birthday only failed for April.

Back along the platform by a trolley full of luggage April stands, cold, thin legged, born prematurely, underweight and still small for her age, holding in one hand a brown paper carrier bag with string handles. Under the other arm, a rubber doll. While June walks on to establish her place at the head of the passport queue in the customs shed, saying to herself that now the journey has really started perhaps four children on one passport is as many as anyone could wish for. More than four—say two further Franklins after Roz—would have meant keeping Nanny and, lovely as that would be, how would Nanny have faced up to the journey and the foreign food which will have to be eaten once the ham sandwiches, digestive biscuits and Worcester apples have run out? June opens her shoulder bag and takes out her spectacles case and her spectacles out of the case and puts them on her nose and considers the four names and dates of birth.

May was the month in which April should have come. And May was the name she should have had. "Well why not call her April to go on with?" several people said. And April stuck. It's very cold still sometimes on April's birthday; once it snowed, but this year where they live in Hampshire there was a lovely warm spring day and April's birthday tea

10

was on the lawn with candles on the cake just staying lit, but fluttering.

June in the customs shed puts her spectacles back in their case and in the shoulder bag. This, where she stands, is called a queue; behind her trains and people, and ahead of her the smell of the port and noises of cranes and distant engines. She is used to queues by now, queues for Identity Cards, queues for gas masks, queues for ration books. People say there will be more and more queues for everything in England as the war goes on, but June is going to warmth and plenty where she will not have to edge close behind the person taking a long time in front of her.

She peers at other people's passports, some like hers navy blue and gold with the lion and the unicorn on the front, others small and papery leaflets and not British. Behind her is an English Army officer with a red-banded cap who may be a Brigadier or perhaps a Colonel, but identification of army ranks is not what June is good at. Behind him a man in a bowler hat is carrying a brief case; not every man wears uniform in December 1939.

She turns and looks back along the customs shed for the trolley which should appear in the wide opening soon. The wind blows from the dockside through the shed and out at the platform end. Someone on the train said they were in for a choppy crossing. The passport queue moves forward: June says to the Army officer behind her, "Do go in front of me when it comes to my turn. Coping with queues is such a business, isn't it? Heaven knows what's happened to my children."

"Can I help you? Can I go and look for them?"

"Oh no. I wouldn't dream of it. How kind." She turns to the wide opening and still sees no sign of the children or of the trolley. "How kind." She goes on looking. "How very kind, but I don't see why you should."

The army officer picks up his suitcase and turns towards the back of the queue.

"How awfully kind. I'm afraid they are a terrible rag bag."

11

"How many of them are there?"

"Just four ... no five ... because there is the Swiss Governess."

The officer lifts his leather suitcase and walks away along the queue and down the shed and June hears the train getting steam up to move away from the platform, and hears the doors slamming and explains to the man in the bowler hat that he may go next, but that, if her family arrive, she would like the place after him. Then she smiles at the French woman who comes next and says the same in fairly fluent French, which it is nice to have a chance to practise even before the English Channel has been crossed.

They do not know which port this is. They reached it from Victoria Station and the cliffs are white, but all along the line station names were obliterated, which is a war-time ruse by the Government to prevent German spies finding their way round England. She explained this to the children who said that they knew all that already and that a properly equipped German spy or parachutist would have a map or have been trained in England before the war. Sandy and Pru faced each other in the carriage and argued whether all spies were parachutists or whether all parachutists were spies. June said that she had decided that in future she would never try to tell them anything because they always knew more about it than she did, which was very tiresome.

Pru was fifteen at the time. Height five foot four, brown hair, green eyes.

Sandy, thirteen at the time, five foot two, sandy hair, grey eyes.

April, nine, four foot exactly, blonde hair in plaits, grey eyes.

Roz, seven at the time, three foot eleven, brown hair, green eyes.

Pru (statistics, extra), bust 36″, waist 24″, hips 36″.

Whatever the name of this port, they now walk towards the ship which towers above them on full tide. June goes in front

12

holding April by the hand. June and April are the spearhead of the Franklin party and are flanked by Pru and Sandy who come slightly behind and far apart from each other. Mademoiselle walks with Roz at the back, keeping pace with the trolley full of luggage which is pushed by two porters, avoiding the train and crane rails on the dockside.

June: The wind blows her hair up round her hat, hair which is called brown on the passport, but which is duller than brown and darker than blonde, thin and straight and for which she has a permanent wave every two months or so. On board she will find a hair net out of her shoulder bag and put on a headscarf.

April, whose thin hand she holds, wears, like Pru and Roz, a spruce green Harris tweed overcoat with velvet collar, also dark green kneesocks. But April also wears a Shetland patterned woollen Tam o' Shanter pulled down over her ears against the wind. April has worn warm hats with her plaits sticking out at stiff angles from them ever since she had pneumonia about the time of Munich. She takes small quick steps to keep up with June and to avoid the luggage trolley which has caught up close behind her heels.

The luggage trolley: contains two leather trunks, two canvas holdalls (leather strapped, one green, one red), and twelve assorted suitcases. That makes sixteen pieces of luggage.

Sandy, in black overcoat and long grey flannel trousers, puts his hands in his pockets and walks watching his feet carefully, taking care to move parallel with the metal rails sunk into the quay. Pru walks turning her head towards the ships they pass where soldiers in battledress lean over the rails and shout and wave. Pru waves back and walks on, glad that her hair is out of plaits, but wondering how people whose hair has been cut and set in a pageboy style keep it neat and stylish in sea breezes, and hoping that there is a solution which does not include having a perm like her mother's which goes frizzy at a touch of wind and rain. But Pru does not now look at her mother who sets the pace along the quay as if the ship would leave in half a second and as if it would not wait for them as ships nearly always do. Pru

13

walks, rather, as if she were alone; she should have chosen Sandy's side of the trolley so that she could wave and smile at the soldiers without Sandy noticing. At least six soldiers wave and whistle, which makes that twelve waves and whistles from servicemen of various forces since this morning at Victoria. But can she be sure that they are waving at her and not at Mademoiselle who has dark wavy hair and large brown eyes but thicker legs than Pru? Pru slows down to walk beside Mademoiselle and Roz, then slows still more until she is in the rearguard of the Franklin party. Now, if soldiers cheer over rails of troop-ships and go on cheering after Mademoiselle has passed, they are undoubtedly cheering, whistling and waving at Pru herself. That proves it, as Roz would say.

Her mother accelerates, which is hard on the porters with the sixteen pieces of luggage to push and shiny metal rails to be avoided, and hard on Mademoiselle with Roz to drag. If her mother does not slow down, Mademoiselle and Roz will be left behind, and if her mother does not slow down, one of the sixteen pieces of luggage—one of the holdalls balanced high on trunks on the Southern Railway trolley—will fall off. If her mother is going to accelerate like this on all stations and ports all the way to Gibraltar, the journey is going to be completely spoilt. Already her mother, by rushing headlong off to the customs shed, has nearly ruined this part of the journey by upsetting Mademoiselle who had a passport to show as well, by leaving Mademoiselle to deal with both the porters and with April being sick. Not to mention the embarrassment for the Army officer who arrived just as April coughed and spluttered and missed the beach bucket which was brought with them for that purpose.

Pru said to her mother when they caught up with her in the customs shed: "Honestly, Mummy!"

"What's wrong?"

"Well—just honestly ... poor Mademoiselle."

"I don't know what you mean ..."

"And it was frightfully embarrassing for the major or colonel or whatever he was ..."

14

"I'm sure he's used to that sort of thing. I expect he has children of his own ..."

"Well, honestly, how can you be sure? Honestly."

June pushed through customs and got up speed along the quay, dragging April and saying that at least if April had been sick already, she was unlikely to be sick again from seasickness. Pru came behind her. "I just hope we don't see that army officer ever again in all our lives."

"Oh no, darling. I think it's rather nice getting to know people on long journeys."

Pru waited for the luggage to start rolling from the customs shed and fell in beside it, first running a hand down the back of her hair to make sure the pageboy set curled evenly under on her shoulders. Let her mother gallop if she felt she must. At school everyone, with very few exceptions, feels like this about their mothers. But at least Pru prevents her sometimes from making a complete fool of herself, tells her when she wears colours that don't go together and when her lipstick is on crooked and her powder on too thick.

They have now reached the gangway of the Southern Railway Channel steamer which will ferry them across to France, to port unknown, and which will land them alongside the appropriate train which will carry them to Paris, Gare du Nord. At the bottom of the gangway June stops at last and raises her clear voice above the engines of cranes and ships, of footsteps and sailors' voices and gives orders to Mademoiselle and her family to go on board.

On the gangway you step over thin slats of wood. It runs up between blue/green canvas sides. Roz and April go first, holding the polished rail and each carrying brown paper carrier bags with their names on. APRIL in royal blue and ROZ in red. Mademoiselle follows them with the picnic basket. Sandy has a small brown despatch case which was once his father's. Pru has a bright green writing case with her initials on it, P.J.F. in gold. She also has a shoulder bag, her first bag, first adult bag, a piece of grown-up equipment which does not really go with the green knee socks and childish green tweed coat, but, in her suitcase, which is being

15

unloaded from the trolley and brought up behind her on the gangway, she has three pairs of stockings, silk ones, which she will wear as often as possible from now on and which would have been nice to have been wearing as she walked along the quay.

The gangway, where they step on and over wooden slats, is steeply pitched with the ship riding on such a high tide, and its canvas sides blow towards and away from them in the wind, but they will know the familiar feeling under their feet as they reach the top of it with bags and baskets.

Where they come from, further west along the south coast of England, is also by the sea, a flat place east of Portsmouth but not quite in Sussex. Elm trees grow there very tall and the flat fields are for hay or grazing dairy cows. A watercress stream leads down to a muddy neck of the Solent Water. The Franklins' house, a farm, a cemetery and a church stand isolated between the water and the main road. Here buses run, green buses, east to west and west to east but you can only sometimes hear the traffic and sometimes train whistles from the main south coast railway line. That place is where they left for London yesterday via Petersfield, Guildford and Woking.

June walks out of the glass-protected part of the upper deck and into the open air on the wide stretch of deck on the bows of the Channel steamer. She is bulky because she is wearing her camel-hair coat belted over her coat and skirt, and she wears an emerald green square scarf tied over her hairnet and underneath her chin. She takes the white-railed companion-way even higher to the boat deck, where the wind blows and from where, beyond white rails, there is only a view of grey-green sea into which the bows of the steamer plunge and rise.

She turns and leans on the following wind which helps her walk towards the stern. The tower of the dock of the unknown port is still in sight between white cliffs.

"Goodness it is rough!" she would shout if there were anyone else on the boat deck to hear her voice. She has walked before like this on boat decks, following on liners to places in the Empire where Dawson went on battleships. This could have been a long sea voyage for all the family. What fun. But now there are magnetic mines and U boats, but none here surely on this short crossing when they will be in France by lunch time.

Going forward again lurching against the wind, she sees coming up the companion-way and clinging to the rails of it the figure of Roz, coat blowing, hair stiff in salt wind, eyes half closed.

June shouts: "Where's Mademoiselle? Why did you leave her, Roz?"

"I didn't. She left me. She's gone to the lav with April."

"April's not being sick again, I hope."

"No, but Mademoiselle is, probably."

"Oh well, that's all right then," June shouts. Then shouts again: "Poor Mademoiselle; we ought to go back down again."

Roz's hair is thick and straight and was cut short last week, not quite as short as a boy's which was what Roz wanted, but very cropped and very straight which makes her face look squarer than it was. "None of us are ever seasick, are we?" she calls out as the ship climbs up a wave.

"I have been once."

"Was it rougher than this?"

"Oh yes, much rougher."

"This isn't rough really, is it then?" Roz puts both feet on the bottom of the boat deck rails and leans out to face towards the coast of France.

"It's better," her mother says, looking in the same direction, "to stay in the fresh air if you can bear the wind."

"I can always bear the wind."

"You've grown up so much, Roz, since Nanny left."

"I'll stay here all the way to France." She moves one foot to another rail and looks down on the lower deck. The ship

17

slides down the wave and June reaches out an arm. "You don't need to hold me. I don't need to be held." She lifts her face and balances on the rail as the ship reaches the pit between the waves, and knows that she has sea legs which not everybody has.

A sailor comes up the companion-way beside them, wearing yellow oilskins, but underneath this Roz can see that he is not a proper sailor but only a railway channel steamer sailor. He shouts something at her mother which neither of them can hear above the wind, but her mother answers. "Yes. Very nice thank you." He comes nearer and can be heard to say: "Is the little one all right? Bit of a swell for her, I'd say."

"Oh no. She likes it."

"No fear," Roz shouts, "I like it."

"They make kids tough these days." He goes along the boat deck, head down against the spray, towards the stern, and Roz calls to her mother that sea legs are just a matter of knowing when the bows are going up and when the bows are going down. It is not frightening, this sea, like seas which roll high above your head on beaches, because you are above this sea and above the waves.

The sailor who went aft comes forward, passing them again and nodding at them both. Roz watches him go down the companion way. Perhaps he might just guess she is the daughter of an Admiral and he might just guess that usually when she goes on board it is on board a ship commanded by her father, and that she goes in the Admiral's Barge which has seats in it like seats in a First Class Railway Carriage, and comes alongside to the sound of bosuns' pipes and orders being shouted.

"We must go below now, Roz."

But you must never tell people what your father is, unless they ask you specially. That would be boasting to tell them what he is. You can only hope that people guess.

Sway on the rail, let one foot leave the rail. Let one foot leave the rail, and then the other, balance above the ocean

18

on your stomach, humming to yourself, but not your mother, the tune of the band of the Royal Marines.

'A Life on the Ocean Wave' is what they play on Navy Days and other occasions on the parade ground at Whale Island in Portsmouth, with the sun shining on trumpets, cymbals, tubas and euphoniums, and flashing on the huge brass spiky baton which the man who leads them throws into the sky and catches after it has twirled. You hear them drumming before they come; they come first just drumming, and between drum-rolls they jerk their drumsticks up to the brims of the wide white hats out of which brass spikes rise, marching out from under the archway of the barracks and seen by the Admiral's family in the front seats of a temporary stand or from the balcony of a dockyard office. After the drumming, the brass begins and the tune comes nearer across the air as they march towards the stand until finally they are playing at your feet. 'A Life on the Ocean Wave', with round mouths of brass close up and with the beat and throb of the largest drum worn on the stomach of the drum major, carrying pulsating waves through the ground and up the stand or building, shaking and tingling through your feet, and beating.

"Come down now, Roz."

Once they went to an outdoor church service where they sang hymns accompanied by the Marines, voices coming from all directions round the square, unevenly in waves and not quite in time. 'Eternal Father Strong to Save Whose Arm Hath Bound The Restless Wave'. Then prayers from the chaplain, who is also a Lieutenant Commander, standing on a carpet on the tarmac reading 'In The Beginning Was The Word'.

Roz sways on the rail above the restless wave which seems unbounded. In the beginning was herself and no-one else. There were others born before her in the huge bed where her parents sleep. And at the end of the service they sang 'All People Who On Earth Do Dwell' which her father sings his loudest, being the Old Hundredth and his favourite hymn. It was all something to do, that service last year was something to do with there not being a war after all. And now there is

19

one, which must have made the person who thought of having the service feel a bit silly.

It was also the service where it is said that April caught pneumonia, which is why she stays below on a deck chair with her Tam o' Shanter on and cannot come on to the top deck of all just below the funnel which blew as they left the harbour and now blows again and is just about the loudest noise you've ever heard.

This morning it was night in London as they stood on Victoria Station and took their gas mask cases off their shoulders and handed them to their aunt. Gas bombs, it seems, may well be dropped in England, but not on France or Spain or on Gibraltar.

"But gas can blow from England southwards," said Roz.

"Of course it can't," her mother said.

At home on the nursery door Mademoiselle painted a poster which said "*Et votre* gas mask" which meant that you never left for school or anywhere without the square box thumping with sharp corners on your back. The mask itself, once tried on, is never taken out except for practice. Inside the mask smells of rubber and has black metal holes in the bit which comes under your chin. Inside the mask you hear your own breathing. The mask is said to keep people alive for several hours, by which time, everyone says, of course the gas has blown away. If Roz had been a few years younger they would have had to get a kind of box in which to put her during gas attacks, about the size of a rabbit hutch, her mother says.

In the beginning was herself and no-one else, either in a rabbit-hutch-sized gas mask or in the rubber face mask or riding a bicycle down the drive at home or listening to the service and the band of the Royal Marines or being born in record time on the wide bed one August when her mother is said not to have even got her shoes off so quick was the birth. A record, maybe, but not for Roz to boast about, they keep on saying.

"Of course we will win the war," her mother said, the Sunday it broke out.

"How can you tell?"

"Well, of course we will."

"That's boasting."

Fifteen minutes they said she was born in, from the moment her mother, walking in the garden in a heatwave wearing beach pyjamas, decided Roz was coming. But this may be a case of boasting also. It does not take fifteen minutes to get from the garden to the bedroom. It takes about three minutes if you run and half a minute at the most to get your shoes off, once you are on that bed. It has been tested. Probably her mother lied about the shoes. Or lied about the time. Sometimes she says "the other day" and means last month or several months ago. Sometimes she says "in a few minutes" which means probably not for hours and hours. She is equally wrong when she says "you might fall into the sea" when everyone knows that is impossible if you are holding on to the top rail with two hands and have two feet firmly on the lowest rail, and if you watch the waves coming up under you and the ship you are on going down again and the next wave and the one after that and the one following and the one following that, Channel waves all the way to France.

That was all long ago, that was, being born in the room which looks over the lawn, the flagstaff, the hayfield this side of the lane to the main road. The beginning of the war was quite long ago as well, when there was Sandy's ridge tent on the lawn outside and people listening to the wireless inside and coming out through the garden door to say the war had started.

"What did they say had started?" Roz asked inside the tent.

Being at war seemed hardly at all different. The sun stayed out, some planes flew over but they were English and the farmer came as usual to drive the cows from the paddock to the milking shed.

Grey skies and spots of rain and huge but not really dangerous seas. June holds the half-belt at the back of Roz's coat with

21

one gloved hand and the ship's rail with the other. What else can one do with children in wartime? The Collinsons sent all theirs to a grandmother in Penzance, the Wesley-Smiths risked magnetic mines and sent their ten and twelve year old by sea to cousins in Connecticut, and Audrey Wesley-Smith went with them. The Painters' son has been evacuated with all his prep school to the Bahamas, but Dawson and June Franklin don't believe in doing that; they take theirs with them. If we go, we go together, don't we? And Gibraltar will be lovely, won't it?

Half way to France. June wears around her waist, over her vest, but underneath her jersey, a suede money belt with pockets in it, containing altogether one hundred pounds in British sterling.

At least half way to France. June clutches at Roz's coat. Her sister Kay sent her baby, Charlotte, with Nanny looking after her, to spend the war at Nanny's sister's house in Petersfield.

What June and Dawson always say is that we all sink and swim together, rather sink or swim together. They always say that and they always have and everything has been all right so far, except for what might be called a narrow squeak when April had pneumonia after Munich.

No. Or no fear as the children would say, you do not stay apart from them for long. And at Gibraltar there is this house, this garden, these naval servants, cooks and stewards, these horses, dogs, this school. And the duration of the war, as it is coming to be called, could well go on for donkey's years as Nanny used to say.

Beside her, Roz's voice demands how far it is to France. "Not far."

"It's lucky they are on our side, the French."

Watch how the water streams over and off the bows as they rise from a wave. Hold on to Roz with driving gloves and hold on to the rail. See how the water down there close in to the ship looks black with bubbles rising, floating. France may be near but the horizon is not far and the view from the boat deck ends in cloud.

22

"The Dutch are on our side, the Belgians and the Danes aren't they?"

"Oh yes, I'm sure they are."

Another ship is in the Channel, coming up beside them from the south. A narrow hull, and could be a destroyer, but its superstructure is in the rainclouds.

"That's not a German ship?"

"Of course it isn't, darling."

It's definitely a destroyer. June can see its guns and bridge, its depth charges in the stern as it comes nearer.

"Norway? Sweden's neutral and so is Switzerland but there's all the colonies and dominions."

"Yes of course there are."

Warships in the war are camouflaged, not grey, not signalling or wearing flags, but anonymously steaming, coming out of rainclouds, ready to raise guns, escorting ships across the Channel.

"All the colonies and dominions, all the Empire and their soldiers, all their sailors. And what about the Americans?"

In peacetime warships anchor in the Solent dressed over-all for Jubilees and Coronations and to be inspected by the King.

"The Americans might send us weapons, I suppose," says June.

"What about the Russians?"

The destroyer ploughs its way, not seeming to rise and fall with waves, heading, overtaking, low in the water, guns uncovered, heads on bridge, smoke from its funnels scudding back to England.

"I think the Russians have a pact with Germany."

June and Roz stand and there are lifebelts on the rail on either side of them and watch the ship go past. You could not well be safer, could you, anywhere than on a boat deck of a British Channel steamer with a ship of the Royal Navy close at hand.

This morning in the blacked out morning at Victoria, June kissed her sister Kay. Kay works in the Ministry of Information and has always worked in London, wears black coats and skirts, silk stockings, always high-heeled shoes. "How brave you are, my darling," she said as she kissed June back.

"Oh, I don't know," said June.

Kay ran beside the train, still waving on the platform, carrying their gas masks, having given everybody presents for the journey. Very generous. Kay's elegant shins flashed on the platform.

June raises her chin into the wind and watches the stern of the destroyer, takes Roz's hand.

Kay said: "I'll miss you all so much; you've no idea."

"But you've got Charlotte."

But Charlotte is in Petersfield with Nanny, learning to walk in Nanny's sister's tiny house. And Kay has Bernard whom she lives with.

"Give my love to Nanny," June called out, last thing at Victoria.

"And Bernard sends his love," called Kay.

"How nice of him. Give all our love to Nanny, don't forget."

It could be just as brave to stay in London if you like that kind of life and send your only child away from you. And Kay has Bernard who is a poet. Kay, once widowed, once divorced, must be quite happy on the whole, because she is a writer too, has written novels, worked in publishers. That sort of life, thinks June. That sort of life. And she screws up her eyes against a dash of spray and wonders if the luggage is all right.

So generous of Kay; she brought them books to pass the journey. For June she brought a book of Bernard's poems.

Down there in the luggage there are winter clothes and summer clothes and riding clothes and swimming clothes. There can't be anything you have forgotten. Passport, visa, lists of addresses and telephone numbers in case you should have trouble anywhere like Paris or Madrid, tickets, wallet, money belt.

June cannot but wonder who could think of poetry at a time like this.

At Gibraltar there will be, as well as servants, horses, dogs, the Apes, of whom it is said, if they die off or leave the Rock then British Rule will fail.

June wrote poetry once and still has it in soft-backed leather notebooks, kept in the bottom drawer of her walnut bureau which stands under the south window of the drawing-room at home. She keeps her poetry books in the same drawer as her photograph albums which are numerous. She looked at Bernard's poetry on the train. "It's about war," said Pru. "About the Spanish Civil War and very *avant garde*."

On the boat deck of the steamer in her emerald green head-scarf, June forgets about poetry and about Bernard but remembers the walnut desk.

"You don't like it, do you?" Pru said on the train.

"Not awfully on the whole."

"You just can't cope with anything *avant garde*."

"I just don't think war is a very nice thing for people to write poems on."

The children said Bernard was quite decent really, not wet or soppy; he called Kay honey-bunch and sweetie-pie and knew people in the B.B.C. and was important.

On the boat deck she pulls Roz off the rail and says that they must go below now, that Roz must go and sit with April and Mademoiselle because June is going to find Pru and Sandy and make sure that the luggage is all right.

Kay's present to Roz was also poetry, but with pictures: *Flower Fairies of the Wood*, a poem and a picture for each fairy, the Bluebell Fairy, the Fairy of the Anemones, the Little Elf of the Celandines. Roz opened it on the train, took one look and stuffed it to the bottom of her carrier bag.

She sits on the deck chair on the covered deck, her carrier bag beside her. Spray splashes on the glass in front, and Mademoiselle and April lie back in their chairs, faces pale and with eyes closed. They did not even notice her arrival.

Roz takes out the fairy book and holds it on her knee, stiffening as the ship lurches. She will not read it. Only look at it. It would be better thrown overboard but you never do things like that with presents. April's present was grown-up poems like the Ancient Mariner and the Lady of Shalott and was leather with a silk ribbon for a bookmark. It is there on April's lap while April herself, like Mademoiselle, breathes deeply with her eyes closed.

A wave breaks on the window. People walk past the deck chairs clutching the bulkhead rail and looking straight ahead of them or carefully at their feet.

April should have had the fairy book. April believes in fairies or says she does, but this may be because she is polite and knows that some people think it is nice for children to believe in fairies.

The only decent fairy in the book is the Imp of the Willow tree who has dark curly hair and brown eyes like Mademoiselle. Roz holds the book carefully open on her knees and sees how through the window sometimes you can see the sky and sometimes only grey-green sea, and feels how sometimes you are leaning back on the chair and sometimes tipping forwards almost out of it.

Mademoiselle sighs and April sighs and as the sea comes into sight, Mademoiselle's knitting and April's poetry book slip from their knees and slide on to the deck and across to rest against the bulkhead. Roz grips the book and goes on looking at the picture where the Willow Imp dims and blurs and she has to breathe deeply to go on looking.

Now sky now sea. Pretend you cannot see them. Pretend as people pass that you are reading. Here is the Army Office struggling past, who came on to the platform when A₁ was sick this morning. Watch his polished shoes go past, do not look up. And turn a page. Just now was sea and now there's sky again.

The Bluebell Fairy looks a bit like April looked when she went as a fairy to a fancy-dress party. Except for the plaits, it looks like April. Roz went as a policeman, but at the party it was Roz who was sick, not April. Now sky now sea. Roz shuts the book and stands on the sloping deck, then walks slowly and looking straight ahead of her to the door which she pushes open and which swings in the wind behind her.

All wild out here but safe against the rail, both sea and sky in view. Gulps of fresh air and cold spray in your face again and this must be the place to be. This is the place where never to be sick, where you can stand with your back to the Army officer as he walks on deck and with your back to people huddled in rows on wooden seats. This is the stern of the boat, the after deck, and there is a gap between one of the seats and the rail where, on a pile of ropes, a sitting place is found. April is sick in cars and trains and buses and by Army Officers' feet on platforms.

Watch the white wash of bubbling froth the steamer makes behind. Eternal Father Strong to Save. But better forget the Restless Wave. Think of the fairies in the wood. No, think of something else. There is a Green Hill Far Away is better. Open your mouth to sing but not be sick. All People That on Earth do Dwell as sung to the band of the Royal Marines. And remember that you have sea legs. It's nearly Christmas; Hark the Herald Angels Sing.

It may be boasting to say you are never sick, however. It is true to say that you are hardly ever sick and it would be true to say that April is sick more often. It would also, therefore, be true to say that you are a better traveller than April, but people would say that was boasting too. Boasting can be true sometimes in that case. Hark the Herald Angels Sing, Mrs Simpson's pinched our King. Supposing the Germans say they will win the war and someone says "You're boasting". Oh God our Help in Ages Past. Someone will turn out to have been boasting untruthfully in the end. Roz turns up the velvet collar of her green tweed coat and pulls her knee socks right up over her knees to meet the coat.

June found Pru and Sandy on the same deck level as Mademoiselle and April, but facing port not starboard, facing down the Channel where it widens towards Lands End and the Atlantic, on deck chairs with their writing cases beside them. She asked them if they were all right and went to see the luggage on the lower deck and went back up again to where she had stood earlier with Roz. Where she stands now watching France get nearer, sandy beaches edged with tufty grass and beyond low buildings of a town which may be Calais or Dunkirk or Boulogne perhaps, coming towards her on the boat deck.

She asked Pru and Sandy if they were all right and they said yes of course they were, so she went on past them to the bows and up the companion-way. They looked exhausted. No wonder, because Kay had taken them out to a show with Bernard and they said they had had dinner afterwards, with wine. June spent the night at a nice quiet old-fashioned hotel near Victoria with Mademoiselle and the little ones.

Very kind of Kay of course. Very generous of Kay to have them to stay, to spend all that money, to have Pru's hair done, to buy Pru bust bodices that Pru has been wanting and saying for months are worn by everyone at school. And to buy Pru silk stockings, high heeled sandals and two cotton frocks at Selfridges.

Pru, without plaits for the first time for ten years and with an emphasised bust, lies, legs crossed on a deck chair two decks down. June stands with both hands on the boat deck rail, facing the bows of the steamer which are aimed at the opening between two piers of this French port.

It says on her passport that she was born in 1901. (In June of course). And she did write poems once. She left them in a drawer with photographs in the bureau where she writes letters and pays bills every morning and where she has taught four children to read and write before they went to school. *Reading Without Tears* four times over through book one and then book two, with Nanny upstairs in the nursery, a cook in the kitchen, a parlour maid and housemaid carpet-sweeping and silver polishing throughout the morning. June will have clever, educated children, much better educated than herself, top in everything at school and knowing longer words. And then, after lessons, there was lunch and, after

lunch, gardening or going out to meetings of the Mothers'
Union or the Women's Institute or tea with friends. At the
end of the day, after afternoon tea that is, there were card
games, Happy Families, Old Maid, Rummy in the drawing-
room, or, for the little ones when they were very little ones,
singing nursery rhymes for which June could play the grand
piano by the window which looked out on to the garden,
after which the children used to go to bed and Dawson
came home if his ship was berthed at Portsmouth, and that
was that until quite recently.

June can drive a car, play tennis well enough for tennis
parties, plan a dinner party menu and order the ingredients.
Can make speeches at Women's Institutes, Mothers' Unions,
open fêtes and sing clear soprano at all times in church.
Writes letters full of news to a great many friends and even
more relations. People never dislike June; she is what she
would call easy on hand, enthusiastic and full of admiration
for whatever is offered her on any social or ceremonial occasion. Energetic. Walks fast as has been seen, weeds the
garden fast, talks fast at parties and nearly everywhere, talks
clearly, conversation full of anecdotes of times remembered
by herself and people she knows well.

She stands on the boat deck of the Channel steamer and
wonders if she can complete this journey.

Her clothes are mostly pink and blue, her chintzes on her
chairs and sofas flowery. She likes plain walls, patterned
carpets and lavender dried in china bowls. Plays games with
children, laughs a lot and never minds losing. At least she
never shows it if she does. Has never mastered Contract
Bridge. Her favourite games: charades, dumb crambo and
any acting game. Drawing-room comedy means exactly that
to June. Sleeps well at night and always says her prayers.

Her children say she laughs too loudly, eats too fast and
when she is out in a street with them she makes remarks
about people passing. They really know that she knows perfectly well that ugly people and people with silly voices are
to be pitied and not laughed at, but in that case she should
not laugh at them. She herself is far from ugly; in fact you'd

29

say she was good looking, even beautiful, they've heard it said.

Her favourite drink: champagne. Her second favourite drink is sherry. Her favourite food: roast chicken, bread sauce, sprouts and roast potatoes.

Her children say she talks too loud. They also say she can be very spiteful and does not bother with people she does not want to bother with. They say she is dismissive as when she remarks that people say "Pardon" or "Toilet" which people cannot help. They think she sings too loud in church but are very glad that it is in tune. She pushes forward to the front in wartime queues, in queues for tea at garden parties, even those held at Buckingham Palace. Not that her children have seen her do that, but their father has told them that she does.

She sings as she weeds the garden or grooms the children's ponies. Takes very small children by the hand to play Old Macdonald's Farm or Oranges and Lemons. Favourite dances: quick waltz and Scottish reels. She bounces as she dances.

When they are critical of June, she says: "Oh you are so critical, you children," and knows that it is because of their intelligence and their better education.

June's husband: Dawson Franklin, Vice Admiral, R.N., acting full Admiral for the Gibraltar posting. Letters after his name: K.C.V.O., C.S.I., C.M.G. and more. People describe him: witty, charming, or, if it is a woman who describes him, witty, charming and attractive.

He has commanded destroyers, cruisers, battle cruisers, battleships. In one of these he fought at Jutland. The ship in front of him and the ship behind him were both sunk, but his ship survived. Spent time on shore postings, such as the Admiralty in London where he wore a bowler hat, pin-stripe suit and carried an umbrella. He had quite neat dark curly hair before going rather bald.

His children know him to be brave; he can be fierce with them. They know him to be funny, very funny. His jokes are funny even when you've heard them ever since you can remember. There's a very funny one about King George V.

Some photographs of Dawson: white summer uniform, standing in Malta or Singapore or on the deck of one of his commands, usually holding his telescope slung between two hands. Early photographs show one row of medals, but now four are seen. The gold braid bands are mounting on his cuffs, three narrow ones, then four, then one very thick one, then another narrow and another and another.

An Admiral's flag is like the white ensign but without the Union Jack in the top right hand corner. An Admiral's flag, for that matter, is like St George's flag. An Admiral starts off as a Rear Admiral, and his St George's cross, red on white background, is distinguished by red dots in three of the four quarters. A Vice Admiral loses one of these and a Full Admiral loses two. An Admiral of the Fleet loses all three and flies St George's flag unblemished on ship or car or on official residence. An Admiral of the Fleet becomes a baron usually with a title for his son to inherit. Dawson's son, Sandy, has not thought about this, but the Franklin children generally expect that every now and then their father will be promoted.

He flew his Vice Admiral's flag from 1935 onwards on His Majesty's yacht *Victoria and Albert*, which spent most of its time in Portsmouth Dockyard but was taken out in Navy Week and on occasions when the monarch was to review the fleet or visit Scotland.

There are photographs of Dawson following up the gangway of the *Victoria and Albert*, three successive Kings, in 1935, in 1936 and again in 1937. The last of these three kings stammered, as is known, but during an early voyage to Scotland in Coronation Year, he asked Dawson to kneel down on the deck of the anchored ship in the Firth of Forth and was handed a silver-bladed sword by one of his equerries. Dawson was asked to kneel on a red velvet cushion and to rise Sir Dawson Franklin, K.C.V.O. The story is that it was a complete surprise, but it must have been possible to guess what was about to happen. It must be possible to guess what is about to happen if a king who stammers, and does not

31

usually carry a sword, reaches for one or asks someone to run and fetch one from wherever swords are kept on early summer Coronation trips round the Scottish coast.

Sandy stammers sometimes like the King, and April, also like the King, cannot say her Rs. It cannot have been "Rise Sir Dawson" and must have been "Wise Sir Dawson". Whichever it was, the Franklin children assume it was deserved. The older ones know that they would rather have a father who earned a title than a father who was born with one.

Sandy sits on the enclosed port lurching deck of the Channel steamer trying to read the *Daily Telegraph*. He has not been seasick. "*Graf Spee* Scuttled Last Night", he reads from headlines, steadying the paper. "Vast Crowds Watch *Graf Spee* Sail", it says further down. Inside the paper he reads that Commodore Harwood, who led the attack by H.M. ships, *Ajax*, *Exeter* and *Achilles*, has just been knighted.

At Sandy's prep school several people have fathers who are knights. When Sandy's father was knighted Sandy was sent for after P.T. in the gym. The headmaster said: "Good news, Franklin."

Sandy said "Thank you Sir," and went to the changing rooms feeling that he should feel different. His best friend, Budgett, said: "I say, Franklin. Congratulations."

One hundred and thirty German sailors sailed the *Graf Spee* to the spot off the coast of Venezuela where she was scuttled, but it does not say in the *Daily Telegraph* what happened to them afterwards.

Sandy left that school last week, and so did Budgett, but Budgett is going next term to Dartmouth Naval College and Sandy is coming back to England to go to Harrow.

A German officer in the *Graf Spee* lost both his legs and refused to let his men carry him below. As he lay dying on the deck, it says in the *Daily Telegraph*, he only asked to be told how the fighting was.

Sandy is not going to Dartmouth because he is colour blind. If you cannot tell green from red when it is dark and you are at sea, you would not be able to distinguish port lights from starboard lights on approaching vessels.

"All Day Patrols", the *Daily Telegraph* says, are taking place on the Western Front, where increasing signs of liveliness are shown. German and English soldiers have clashed, with heavy losses for the Germans.

Sandy and Budgett took the Dartmouth medical on the same day, choosing numbers made up of orange, pink and red dots. Sandy saw the wrong numbers. It is very difficult, everybody says, extremely difficult, when there are so very many dots, so very many different pinks and oranges and reds. Sometimes he saw no numbers in the dots at all.

"Finns Smash Two Soviet Divisions." Sandy yawns and stretches on his deck chair and stands up to see if the coast of France is yet in sight.

"Air Battle Off East Coast. Crowds See Bomber Dive Towards The Sea."

When people ask Sandy what he is going to be when he grows up, it's rather difficult to say since failing Dartmouth. Sometimes he says it depends how long the war lasts.

"Nazi Sea-Plane Bases Bombed."

In the nursery with Nanny they used to push plum stones to the edge of the plate and count them. Tinker, tailor, soldier, sailor, rich man, poor man, beggarman, thief. Sandy leaves the *Daily Telegraph* on the chair and goes out on the deck. He can see that the sea is greeny grey with white crests on the waves, that the rails of the ship are white and that the deck under his feet is pale wood boards with tar between. But that is not good enough for the Royal Navy and he will just have to be, as everyone says, good at something else.

Last night at the Prince of Wales Theatre he saw, with Pru and Kay and Bernard, *The Gaieties of Montmartre*, with chorus girls called 'The Loveliest in London' who appeared with Gillie Potter who was very funny. One could be like Gillie Potter if one had the wit. One could be an engine driver as little boys are said to want to be. And trains are interesting.

At school they used to talk about model railways and compare notes about train-spotting expeditions they had been on in the holidays. They compared penknives and cricket bats and which public schools they were going to when they left this prep one. Some boys, like Budgett, knew exactly what they were going to be and were going to the right places to train for it.

The chorus girls, the Loveliest in London, wore diamond mesh stockings which went all the way up and did not seem to be kept up by suspenders, which was interesting. The men who danced with them in the chorus may know how the stockings are kept up, and must be men with good excuses not to be in the army, navy or airforce. Being a dancer is not what anyone would consider a good career, however. Tinker, tailor, soldier, sailor; whichever or whatever one will be, one will probably find out about suspenders at some point in life.

Sandy stands out on the deck as the breeze diminishes and one pier of the French port slides into his vision. Somewhere over there, the French train, which it will be interesting to see, is waiting.

TWO

A FRENCH TRAIN is drawn by an engine which is a silver streamlined cylinder. Its blunt funnel is encased in the same bright metal, curved and backwards sloping. The engine driver's cab, which in most trains juts up at the back, is contained in smoothly contoured polished metal, and the whole reminds the person standing on the platform more of a design for an aeroplane than of any rolling stock.

The Franklins, playing talking games, are on their way to Paris.

A French railway carriage stands higher above the platform than does an English railway carriage, but this is not because the carriage is taller than its English counterpart, but because French platforms are lower than English ones. To climb into the carriage there are five steps up, and to arrive inside is to find a wider corridor than you would find in England and plusher seats in the compartment and upholstery in soft browns and beiges, walnut veneer above the seats and silk tassel-ended cords to hold the curtains back.

"I love my love with an A because he is ambitious. I hate him because he is avaricious. His name is Andrew Anderson and he lives in Amiens."

The French railway system has three classes, first, second, third, while the English has only two at present, first and third. The Franklins who travelled third class from Victoria now travel second to the Gare du Nord in Paris.

"I love my love with a B because he is bountiful ..."

On railway stations, French advertisements, French station masters, porters, French public lavatories.

"I love my love with a C because he is charming ..."

French trains shake and rattle in a slightly different rhythm from trains back across the Channel, but after a bit you hardly notice that. Luggage on French railway racks moves in the same way as luggage on English railway racks. French train windows are more difficult to open. French ploughed fields are ploughed the same way as English ones. People begin to play I Love my Love and then stop playing. People go into the corridor and then come back or go to the lav and then come back. April and Mademoiselle knit, Pru writes a letter and Sandy leans forward to hand the *Daily Telegraph* to his mother.

They have rather bigger fields in France.

They all took off their coats because of the heating in the compartment and stowed them on the luggage rack along with bags and basket. But it's still hot. Roz stands up and begins to pull off the Shetland jersey. Her mother puts the *Daily Telegraph* on her knee and leans to help. The jersey is dragged tightly over ears, the buttons catch on strands of hair. Nanny used to say "Skin a rabbit" as she pulled things off you. Roz is left wearing Sandy's old grey aertex shirt, one of his school snake belts holding up her kilt.

April knits a scarf for an airman. She bends her head as she knits and the parting in her hair is as even as the stitches in the scarf; it is like the parting in the Red Sea when the waters were pulled back to let Moses lead the children of Israel out of Egypt. When April knits she puts the needle through the stitch, then she lifts a strand of wool from the ball, winds it round the needle and slowly the new stitch emerges. Her tongue is between her teeth. Slowly the new stitch is made. Either the airman will have been shot down or the war will be over by the time she finishes.

Mademoiselle, next to April, also knits, but so fast and on such tiny needles that you hardly notice she is doing it. She knits herself the white socks in fine wool she always wears. Roz looks out of the window. This is abroad and this is France and, like in England, the telegraph wires swoop and rise between their poles. And swoop and rise again. June from behind the *Daily Telegraph* says how good everyone is being and how smoothly everything is going and just think they will soon be in Paris which is half way to Gibraltar. Sandy says that a quarter of the way would be more accurate. There are tall trees and fields, villages and towns, small groups of houses which would be called hamlets in England. There are bicycles and buses and men in uniform.

French roads go very straight into the distance, and sometimes the fields they go between have no hedges but are lined with tall thin trees. It must be windy the way the tall trees bend together and in one direction. Sometimes a French man bicycles away along a straight French road with a big basket on his handlebars. Sometimes French women can be seen on bicycles with black skirts billowing and black headscarves on their heads; they lean down and pedal hard to get along. It is not raining hard but there are drops from time to time on the windows of the compartment. French clouds are dark grey mostly but sometimes there are streaks of silver white between them; they might move apart to show blue sky.

Interesting things to do on trains in France:

Talking games: I Spy or I Love my Love or Who would you Rather Push Over the Cliff.

Cards: But this French train has no table or flat surface.

Writing games: (can be played on your knee if you and other players have a solid block of paper). Writing games: Heads, Bodies and Legs (except that that is really a drawing game but you have to write a name at the bottom of the drawing.) Real writing games are ones where you write down something and turn the paper over and pass it on. These are—

Wills: Which is where you write down the name of someone who died, what they died of, what they left in their will, to whom they left it and last of all what they want the person they left it to to do with it. It comes out as follows: "The King died of leprosy and left his socks to Mademoiselle to wear on Sunday." Or, "Mr Chamberlain died of smallpox and left a Bible to the man from Thomas Cook to sit on." It can be quite funny.

Consequences is usually funnier: you write down a man's

37

name, then a woman's name and then what he said to her and what she said to him. After that comes what the consequences were and at the end you write down what the world said about it all.

Example of Consequences: Hitler met Queen Mary in the English Channel. He said to her, you haven't cleaned your teeth; she said to him, M.Y.O.B. The consequences were that they got married and the world said Oo la la. That example is a bit feeble. It can be funnier than that. You need a lot of paper, and people have to want to play or it's no good.

French skies are brighter. Clouds are parting. Over the tall thin trees some sunlight comes in a beam and lands on the middle of a road where a French man is bicycling. The beam is moving away from the road and over a ploughed field and then another field. It's like a searchlight but from air to ground. It's moving with the train, a distance from the train, but with it, crossing other roads. More beams of sunlight join it until there is a moving patch of sunlight streaming down which lights up cows on grass and small green hills.

The sun comes through the window. Dust you did not see before is moving in the carriage.

June, reading from the *Daily Telegraph*, says that she sees that there is not going to be any extra butter ration in England for this Christmas. Pru writes a letter to her best friend at school; her best friend is called Oenone. Sandy reads a book and June says that it's very exciting isn't it, about the *Graf Spee* and Commodore Harwood being knighted.

Particles of dust because the sun is shining in; there may be dust all over the world but no-one sees it when it's cloudy.

A conversation in a French train goes like this:

June: "I think young Dickie Forrester was on the *Ajax*. I do hope he is all right. I feel sure he was on the *Ajax*. You remember young Dickie Forrester, don't you, Pru? We met them at the Burneys. He'd be about twenty now."

Another thing to do: if you haven't any cards or any paper and everyone else is knitting, writing letters or reading out of newspapers, is to count up to one hundred, first in English, then in French. And after that decide on the order you like people in your form at school.

Pru says: "I don't remember anyone called Dickie Forrester."

Or, if you have a pencil, draw moustaches on all the Fairies of the Wood except the Fairy of the Willow Tree. Or pick your nose if nobody is looking.

June: "I felt sure you came and met him, Pru, that time at the Burneys in Basingstoke."
Pru: "No, I didn't honestly. I've never even heard of him."

Play I Love My Love on your own to yourself without your lips moving so people won't know you are doing it. And, if they ask, say that you are praying. Say that you are praying for children who are hungry or who are refugees.

June (reading from Engagements in the *Daily Telegraph*): "I see that Daisy MacBryde has got engaged at last. They *will* be pleased."

Or say that you are praying that the war will soon be over, but only because we have won it and not the Germans.

June (turning to back page where births, marriages and deaths are listed): "And old Mr Purkis has died at last. You remember Mr Purkis, Sandy. I took you to see him when you were quite little."
Sandy: "I don't remember it."

There must be other things to do and other things to count and put in order. Say the alphabet backwards and say it faster backwards.

June: "I felt sure I took you. Peacefully in Birmingham. I wonder why he died in Birmingham."

Sandy: "Anyone can die anywhere I suppose."

June: "But he lived in Dorking."

Say a poem, say a hymn, try starting at the beginning of the Ancient Mariner and see how far you get.

Sandy: "Perhaps Birmingham is where people go to die."

June: (turning to the front page of the *Daily Telegraph*): "Oh darling, I don't think so. His wife went off her head you know. I'm so glad to see the Finns are doing well against the Russians."

Roz: "Why did Mr Purkis's wife go off her head?"

June: "I don't know. Why *do* people go off their heads? I'll just have another look at the casualty list. I do hope Dickie Forrester is all right."

Conversations in French trains go on. They are about the war, the Finns and Russians and the casualty lists and how someone in the paper says Italy won't join the war. Casualty lists in papers start with people who have been killed, then they go on to people who are missing but believed killed. Then they list people who are only missing and have probably been taken prisoner. The sun is still out, dust particles still swirling in the air of the compartment where they sit three a side, comfortably on the whole with a plush French railway arm-rest between each seat.

Pru: "Bernard thinks Italy will come into the war."

June: "Who?"

Pru: "Bernard. He says it is inevitable."

June: "Oh darling. I don't think so. Italians are such un-war-like people. Daddy is quite sure they won't want to join in."

Sandy: "The Italians may not want to, but Mussolini might."

April: "Perhaps Mussolini's off his head." She goes on knitting.

40

A long time ago, it seems, they had the picnic of ham sandwiches, hard boiled eggs and apples. They had tea out of the thermos and were told there would be only coffee from now on since French people do not make tea. And the water they will drink from now on will be out of bottles. Because of drains in France.

Make a list of everyone you know who is mad or off their heads: Nanny's cousin's mother who was never quite as others are, but who only had to be put into a lunatic asylum when she was old. A woman Mademoiselle knew once, the aunt of the children she looked after while she was in Italy. Uncle Giles's first wife who went mad in Australia. The woman who used to run the Brownies, but she had religious mania which is different. Admiral Stephenson who killed himself but, being a naval surgeon (and not a proper admiral), he knew how to do it by cutting his veins and arteries and getting into a bath of water. Mademoiselle does not say people are off their heads or mad; she says they are *tutu* or *gaga*.

June: "I'm sure you are completely wrong about Italy, Pru."
Pru: "It wasn't me who said it. It was Bernard."
June: "Oh Bernard. Oh I see. Well I don't much care what Bernard says. Anyway how on earth can Bernard know?"
Sandy: "There's nothing wrong with Bernard. He's quite nice."
Pru: "He *is* in the Ministry of Information after all. He's *only* in the Ministry of Information, and if *he* doesn't know about things like that, then who does? I don't know why you don't approve of Bernard."
June: "I've absolutely nothing against Bernard, personally, absolutely nothing."

Think of everyone you know who is dead or missing: *Dead*: Granny last year, Grandmama the year before, Grandpa and Grandpapa before you can remember so they don't really count because you didn't know them. But other people: Uncle Matthew, Uncle Norman, Uncle Peter, all killed in France in trenches fairly young. Mademoiselle's sister of tuberculosis, Mademoiselle's cousin of typhoid fever, Mademoiselle's friend's daughter of diphtheria, Nanny's sister's little boy from being run over, Nanny's other sister's little boy from falling off a tree he should not have been climbing. A boy Sandy's friend Budgett knew once who drowned in the Lake District and whose body was not found for months. Budgett's uncle (also in a trench), a baby Mavis the house maid had who never really lived.

Sandy: "If Italy came into the war, then Gibraltar could be bombed. At least that is what Bernard said."
June: "Bernard has no right to say things like that."
Pru: "Kay said it too. She agreed with him."
June: "They both should know better than to talk like that in front of children."
Pru: "They weren't talking in front of children. They were telling me and Sandy."
June: "Well, I think it is all very silly and unlikely, and, if you don't mind, I don't want to talk about it any more."

An extra list of animals who are dead: Flora and all the six puppies she should not have had but which were by an Alsatian dog who got through the kitchen window when Flora was tied to the kitchen table. Pru's pony Smokey who died of colic; ponies cannot be sick but his insides got twisted. The ginger kitten which fell into a water butt, the nest of blackbirds in the kitchen chimney. Hundreds of mice in traps.

Pru: "If Gibraltar was bombed if Italy came into the war, we would be sent home wouldn't we?"
June: "I really don't know, Pru. I just don't know."
Pru: "We *would* be."

Missing animals. Flora's puppy from the first litter who was called Freddie and went hunting with the terrier from the farm and never came back. The tabby kitten which could

42

not have gone far you would have thought. A rabbit Budgett
had once.

June: "Pru, I'm getting angry. We're very lucky to be going
    where we're going, and if we're bombed we're bombed.
    You know that, Pru. You know that very well. You know
    that Daddy and I always say that if we are bombed we're
    bombed and if we're mined we're mined and that is that."
Pru: "How jolly nice for us!"
June: "I won't have it, Pru. I just won't have it."
Pru: "Won't have what?"
June: "I won't have you always having to have the last word
    in every argument."
Pru: "I don't want the last word."

Missing people: Aunt Kay's second husband, Uncle Hugo
and a cousin of Nanny's who is probably in New Zealand.

June: "I'm saying nothing more."
Pru: "Then that's all right then."
June: "It's wrong of you in front of the little ones. It's very
    wrong of you."
Pru: "Oh *is* it?"
June: "It's very wrong in any case. Extremely wrong."
Pru: "I see. It's wrong."
June: "Oh Prudence!"

She stands up in the carriage and holds on to the luggage
rack and has that look about her eyes which she had when
April nearly died of pneumonia last year or when Flora had
to be put down when all the puppies died. Or the look she has
in photographs from the album at the bottom of the walnut
bureau which are of herself when young. She is not crying
though. She says she is leaving the compartment and going
along the corridor. She says that she is going to powder her
nose and that she is rather cross. Rather cross on the whole
she says going out and sliding the door shut after her.

* * *

Last night June prayed. Beside the bed in the nice hotel which was near Victoria she knelt and put her palms together and closed her eyes and started with the Lord's Prayer. She always starts like that. Then goes on to the God Bless for all relations and includes in this such people as Nanny and Mademoiselle and friends like the Burneys and the Wesley-Smiths. She used to pray for Alfred Stephenson before he cut his wrists; she prays for Alice Stephenson these nights.

And every now and then she got up from her knees and looked through the list she'd made of things to do before leaving England in the morning.

She prayed the prayer the Mothers' Union had produced especially for the war. And she prayed a prayer for travellers: "Grant us O Lord that those who pass by land and sea and..."

And got up again to make quite sure she had the address of the hotel in Paris they would stay at.

The other prayers she prays are variable. Sometimes at night she simply says Psalm 23 because it is so soothing.

And she wondered if she could be sure that Kay would bring Sandy and Pru on time to the station in the morning.

He maketh me to lie down in green pastures: he leadeth me beside the still waters.

And she should have sent a postcard to Nanny before they left to tell her that their Christmas presents had arrived.

He restoreth my soul; he leadeth me in the paths of righteousness for his name's sake.

And she had promised Pru that she would bring Pru's silver party shoes because Pru had joined them straight from school. And she had forgotten them.

Yes, though I walk through the valley of the shadow of death, I will fear no evil; for thou art with me; thy rod and thy staff they comfort me.

And she walked around the room, barefooted, on the carpet, cleaned her teeth at the fitted basin, brushed her hair and listened to the sound of London's traffic which was distant because her room was on the second floor and this was a

44

quiet and residential street. And got into bed believing that it would be difficult to sleep.

And dreamt that she was at home and walking beside the watercress beds with some of the children but could not be sure which. Nanny was somewhere telling June that her sister was going to Worthing for the day, and Kay was somewhere with her second husband, Hugo. There was a picnic and a lot of birds with brightly coloured feathers flying and Nanny said, "Little birds in their nests agree". The trees were out in leaf but were unusual trees, silver birches probably and the grass was shorter than you would expect for a field, not hummocky, but flat and mown. One of the children said there was a mountain they were going to climb and she was trying to argue with them that this was not Scotland. They said, "Where is it, then?"

It could have been a park, but there were cows. It could have been the New Forest where the ponies eat the grass down short. And someone kept saying that she should not have brought them here if there were no mountains especially as the cricket season had not started, and they told her it was getting dark. She said it was not, because she could still see snowdrops and primroses quite clearly; she had planted them, moreover.

Surely goodness and mercy shall follow me all the days of my life and I shall dwell in the house of the Lord forever.

On French trains you look out of windows and see people going home from working in the fields, walking and in carts drawn by horses, coming towards the railway line on roads and tracks beside canals and over bridges. Winter late afternoon in France is like late afternoon in England where people come in from the garden for tea and cannot go out again afterwards because of dark. Here in the carriage there is a light over every seat switched on, but darkness, as it says in the Bible, all over the face of the earth outside until to-morrow.

Blinds are drawn down and fixed into metal notches on

the windows on both sides of the train. Now they might all
be in a tunnel or in the London tube or anywhere in any
country at any time in history since trains were first invented.

June came back from the lavatory and fell to snoozing in
her corner and Sandy went and stood outside in the corridor
where the light comes from bare blue bulbs. Roz took his
seat next to Mademoiselle. Mademoiselle stopped knitting
and looked down at her. "Where is Sir Henry Rabbit, Roz?"

"In my bag."

"Get him out then."

"He's all right."

"He has not been out of his bag for all the journey."

"He's Okay."

On the luggage rack opposite, Sir Henry's long grey silk
fur ears with pink velvet linings hang over the edge of the
carrier bag. Roz climbs on the seat where she sat earlier
and pulls the bag down from the rack. She draws Sir Henry
Rabbit out of it; his long stuffed legs unfold in the navy blue
uniform trousers, and the gold braid on the sleeves of his
jacket catch the light from the bulb above.

"Keep him out for a little, Roz. Let him see France."

"There's nothing to see. It's dark."

The light shines on Sir Henry's silver silk fur face and
brown glass eyes. Six rows of medal ribbons represent his
decorations and the braid on his sleeve is that of a Full
Admiral.

"Sir Henry does not hold with France," says Mademoiselle.

"*Pourquoi?*"

"He says it is *tout à fait* boring so far."

"But he used to sing the *Marseillaise*."

"Oh he likes French people and he is on their side, but
today he has not had much fun. *Pas de conversation.*"

"*Dommage.*"

"Quel *dommage*, Rozzie."

"*Quel dommage.*"

"*Quel* jolly rotten shame, Sir Henry says." Mademoiselle
takes Sir Henry and sits him on her knee. "*Bien, maintenant.*

46

L'Amiral va parler. He will address his people, *comme ça.*"
She lifts Sir Henry's arm and puts his soft padded fist up to
his eyes in a salute.

"People don't make speeches when they are saluting."

"All right, Rozzie. All right. He need not speak. Put him
back in the bag then, Rosalind."

"No. Let him speak. Please Mademoiselle, let him speak.
S'il vous plaît, je vous en prie."

Sir Henry speaks above the rhythm of the train wheels
while June sleeps in the far corner, Pru writes and April
knits and Sandy leans his back against the window into the
corridor. Sir Henry speaks as he has spoken in the past since
Mademoiselle arrived two winters back. Sir Henry has spoken
less since the war began and no-one expects him to say
much as the train passes closer to Switzerland which
Mademoiselle will not see until the war is over.

"What should he speak about then, Rozzie?"

"The time he took a gun boat up the Thames. Or the time
he climbed the north face of the Portsdown Hills. Or the time
he escaped from cannibals at Petersfield. Or when he fought
in the Boring War."

Sir Henry's gift of speech comes from Mademoiselle but his
clothes from Nanny who made new gold braid stripes around
his cuffs and extra medals every time he was promoted.

"No. Sir Henry feels like singing today. He will sing—
There'll always be *une Angleterre* and *patrie d'espoir et
gloire* or his old school song which goes Marches, marches,
marches to the *salle de classe.*"

"What about *Nous allons étendre notre linge sur la ligne
de Siegfried*?"

"*Bien. Commençons.*"

Sir Henry sings to the rhythm of the train, his body flopped
against Mademoiselle's dark grey coat and skirt, her foot
tapping on the floor of the compartment, her brown eyes
staring at the blank window beside her and reflected back.
"Come on now, Sir Henry says, you will all join in the
chorus."

April stops knitting and joins in. June opens her eyes,

47

smiles and closes them again. Pru stops writing and sucks the end of her fountain pen. The sound of the train wheels make you think the train is moving faster and it begins to rock with the speed and sway so that they bump against each other across the arm rests.

No-one pretends that Sir Henry is anything but a stuffed toy. People like Roz do not play with rabbits like people like April play with dolls, bathing them and putting them to bed. Sir Henry is never to be nursed in the arms or patted on the back or given made up medicines for pretended illnesses.

Mademoiselle has a bright white blouse with a flat collar turned back over the lapels of her dark grey coat-and-skirt. She has black hair, brown eyes and long black lashes. It is said that she is very homesick for Switzerland nearly all the time and, even though Switzerland is neutral, she cannot now go back to it, which must explain the look in her eyes from time to time. Switzerland is a very small country and is half surrounded by Germans now and they could easily invade it in spite of its neutrality. She sings for Sir Henry and with Sir Henry on her knee about the Siegfried line, but you must never talk to Mademoiselle about the Germans much or her sadness which is *tristesse* will turn to silence and she will be considering how very possible it would be for *les sales boches* to go up and over the Alps with tanks and guns.

"Sir Henry is *très heureux* to be seeing Paris, Rozzie, I can tell you."

If you talk too much about Switzerland and Germans, the silence which was *tristesse* turns to *colère* which is anger.

"Sir Henry has had *beaucoup de* gay and funny times in Paris, Rozzie."

No-one has ever said exactly why Mademoiselle did not go back to Switzerland before the war started, but it may be because she thought then that she was going to marry someone English.

"Why isn't Sir Henry married, Mademoiselle?"

"Speak French, Rozzie."

"*Pourquoi?*"

"*Pourquoi* what?"

"Pourquoi Sir Henry *n'est-il pas se marié?"*
"Pourquoi n'est-il pas marié, you mean."
"Pourquoi?"
"Sais pas, Rozzie. *Je ne sais pas.* You have had Sir Henry all his life; you should know." Sir Henry is handed back to Roz and put back in the bag, folded at the waist, his ears still hanging out.

He arrived three years ago in a pink velvet dressing gown and cotton paisley pattern pyjamas. First Nanny made him a grey flannel suit and then the uniform, with gradually increasing bands of gold braid on the cuffs. As an early Christmas present this year, Nanny sent in a parcel a white tropical uniform for Gibraltar.

Mademoiselle knits again, but slowly, not raising her eyes. Sometimes she seems to be sighing, but if you asked her why she was sighing she would deny that she was doing it at all. List of people who are sad: Mademoiselle about Switzerland and probably about the Englishman, Mr Brooxbank, whom she did not marry after all. Pru when Smokey died of colic, everyone when Flora's puppies died and Flora had to be put down. Mummy when Granny died, but not all that much. Aunt Kay, probably, when she lost her first husband, Abraham when he had to kill Isaac or thought he was going to have to.

Mademoiselle has stopped knitting altogether. The knitting lies unknitted in her lap and she still sighs frequently. No-one quite knows whether Mr Brooxbank actually asked her to marry him or not. It would have been very suitable, everybody said, because, like Mademoiselle, Mr Brooxbank does not go to church but is a Quaker.

List of religions: Protestant, Church of England, Chapel, Methodist, Baptist, Hot Gospellers, Evangelists and Roman Catholics. You can change from any of the protestant ones to being a Roman Catholic, but Roman Catholics don't let you change from being one of them to being one of the others, although there is something in between called Anglo Catholic. Quakers are different altogether; they don't have services, sing hymns or say prayers except when they make them up

49

and feel like saying them aloud; they do not fight in wars. Mademoiselle says anyone can be a Quaker, but is not sure what happens if a Roman Catholic wants to be one. She was a Plymouth Brethren (a lot of Swiss people are) before she came to England, but joined the Quakers because it seemed a good idea and there was a Meeting House in Portsmouth.

Nanny was Church of England, but low. Almost Chapel really. One of her brothers was a Hot Gospeller. The only difference in the way Nanny behaved in church was that she did not bow her head in the creed when it came to "I believe in Jesus Christ". She was more against Roman Catholics than many people are.

Mademoiselle is good at knitting, making cakes, making fudge and making jokes. She likes bicycling but not taking people for walks as much as Nanny; she likes going to the cinema, yodelling and wearing slacks. She does not like jokes about Germans or about the Swiss Navy, but otherwise absolutely anything can be a joke. She is five foot six inches and weighs nine and a quarter stones usually.

Things you cannot talk to Mademoiselle about: Germans and Mr Brooxbank. Things you could not talk to Nanny about: Roman Catholics, Kay's friend Bernard and people getting drunk.

Nanny was good at sewing but did not cook. Sometimes she has to cook now for Charlotte because her sister cannot manage all the food. She likes going for walks and meeting other Nannies but has not got to know many of them in Petersfield yet. She doesn't like crucifixes and a lot of noise. She is not as tall as Mademoiselle but never would be weighed or measured.

Mademoiselle will play almost any game on earth as long as she is not sad or sighing or feeling ill. Nanny only used to play the games she knew like Old Maid and Snap. Running games outside she never played because of the bone in her leg. Mademoiselle can run extremely fast; she ran races when she was at University; she was only there a year but she ran against another University. What she was studying at

50

University: Theology. She left because her family was short of money and she had to go and work in Italy.

When Mademoiselle reads aloud she usually makes the story up and it is much funnier than it was written.

Things to do when Mademoiselle is sighing, sad, or not feeling well: Look at your watch and stay quiet for quarter of an hour, after which it is worth speaking to her in French about something she likes, like her favourite film which was *Top Hat* or her favourite film star Fred Astaire. Or hum that you are putting on your Top Hat, hopefully. Then, if she does not answer, you wait another quarter of an hour and, if you are still not doing anything nice, you try again, in French again and, if she is not speaking after half an hour, she will probably be sad, sighing, or not feeling well all day.

At night she will just kiss you but you know she will not mean it.

She is still saving up to go back to University, but since the war began she has stopped talking about it.

French trains are long and dark and rattle through the night, although it is only six o'clock and if it were summer there would be hours of light to come. Sandy came back out of the corridor and sat where Roz was sitting before she moved.

The best talking game there is: Who Would You Rather Push Over The Cliff. It is worth mentioning.

"I don't think anyone wants to play that now, Roz darling."

Three opposite three in the compartment: June, Sandy, Pru on one side, Mademoiselle, Roz and April facing them. June, one leg crossed over the other next to the corridor, leans her head on the French second class cushioned back and sometimes her eyes are open and sometimes they are shut. April opposite her, crosses one bony narrow knee over the other and goes on knitting. Pru, legs similarly crossed and not all that fat, writes on the envelope of Oenone's letter.

"Who would you rather push over the cliff, Mr Chamberlain or Hitler?"

"That's very silly darling. Everyone knows the answer to that."

"Okay then. Who would you rather push over the cliff, Hitler or Mussolini?"

"I wish you wouldn't say Okay, darling. It's very American and common. In any case I'm afraid I'm not playing games just now."

Défense de Fumer it says on a label on the window to the corridor, but no-one smokes in any case.

"Who would you rather push over the cliff, Bernard or Uncle Hugo?"

"I'm afraid I don't know Bernard very well, so it's difficult to say. But I was quite fond of Uncle Hugo, so I'd probably push Bernard on the whole."

"Daddy said he is a sap and a wash-out. He hates him."

"I'm sure he doesn't hate him."

"Well you do if you said you'd push him over the cliff."

"It's only a game, darling. Only a game. It's probably best not to play it about people you hate. There's not many people I hate in any case."

"But you'd push Hitler so you must hate him."

"Yes, well, honestly on the whole I do think I hate Hitler; he's caused such an awful lot of damage."

They sit still and they say the train is getting nearer Paris, but it goes faster and faster, knocking, bumping them against each other. On the luggage rack, Sir Henry's ears sway and flap where they hang out of the carrier bag.

"Then if you can play it about people you hate *and* people you like, then you can play it about anybody."

"Yes darling, I suppose you can, but I don't think it's quite like that."

They are putting knitting away in bags and taking out brushes and combs. June takes her lipstick out of her bag and puts some on her mouth without looking at a looking glass. Mademoiselle combs her own hair and the ends of April's plaits. Pru folds down the flap of her writing case, puts her letter to Oenone in the pocket of her coat. Mademoiselle stands up and reaches for coats from the luggage rack. The train goes just as fast.

"Who would you rather push over the cliff, God or the Devil?"

"That's just silly, Rosalind."

"Abraham or Isaac?"

"You must use real people."

"They are real. They are in the Bible."

"No-one's playing any more. No-one was ever playing." June stands above her with the coat, pushing Roz's arms into sleeves, taking the comb from Mademoiselle and pulling it through her hair. Now they all sit with bags or carrier bags on their knees, books and knitting in the bags, waiting for the train to slow down, moving the blinds an inch or two to see what can be seen of Paris beyond the windows of the train.

"Who would you rather push over the cliff, Jesus Christ or John the Baptist?"

"I've had enough of this, Rosalind. I've had enough." The door into the corridor is slid open and Roz taken by the wrist and pushed out there in the blue light, pushed towards the far side by the blinded windows, told by her mother that she does not know how lucky she is to be here on such an exciting journey, and told by everyone else that she is a twirp, a dope, a baby. The blue bulb along the corridor is round, but seen through tears it gives out sharp points and becomes diamond shaped, then star shaped, then dagger shaped, the shape of all spiked weapons. Blue needles of light stretch from its centre like all points of the compass, through the roof of the corridor into the black French sky, if that is what is above the train, and through its floor to French earth, to the west and the Atlantic and to the east and Switzerland and Germany.

She leans back with her back against the lit carriage and lets her shoes slide across the floor, dusty towards the outer wall of the train, so that her head from inside the compartment will be seen at a lower level while her feet slide.

They took no notice of God and the Devil, Abraham and Isaac so why grab and scream and shout about Jesus and John the Baptist, unless it is because they are in the New

Testament and the others are in the Old. They tell you not to say Okay and Gosh and Blast and Damn and do not let you say Jesus. They say do not say Pardon or Toilet or Costume or Handbag. You can say Hitler, Mr Chamberlain, Mussolini, but not Jesus or John the Baptist. They throw you out of the compartment for saying people from the New Testament when Peter was in trouble for saying he did not even know Jesus three times over.

"Just think," her mother's voice echoes from the other side of the sliding door. "Just think. In exactly five days time we shall be crossing the frontier at La Linea into Gibraltar and meeting Daddy. Just think of that!"

Under the blue light, further down the corridor, an English soldier in khaki battledress stands with his feet, like Roz's, wedged against the side of the train, his forage cap tucked into the strap on his shoulder, his arms crossed.

"I think everything has gone so terribly well so far," June's voice echoes from behind the door.

*　　*　　*

Sunday was always Mademoiselle's day off.

Eight days ago exactly, the Sunday before they left, Roz stood on the nursery window seat looking out over the lawn where the flag hung over frosted grass in the centre of the lawn. June raised the flag herself on Sundays these days since Dawson left a month before. This Sunday, Nanny came to lunch and to say goodbye. Nanny sat in the armchair in the nursery, in the chair she always used to sit in. And on her knee was Charlotte.

Roz saw the lawn, the flagstaff, the drooping flag, the hayfield beyond and then the lane which led to the main road. Nanny was dressing Charlotte in fluffy woolly leggings so that they could all go for a walk before the afternoon got even darker.

It was still and frozen and in the drive which led up to the house you could see the ice on potholes. And Nanny in the nursery was saying that Charlotte was just like Roz used to be at that age, stubborn as a donkey, wanting everything at once and such a hasty pudding. And April by the chair sat on the floor and watched and helped push the leggings up over Charlotte's fat baby legs while Charlotte struggled and Nanny said: "She's such a precious angel, such a treasure just like you two were my treasures."

Downstairs June was writing letters at the walnut bureau. She wrote to Pru and Sandy at school and to Dawson on the Rock to tell them all how plans were going for the journey. She sat in her second best winter tweed skirt, her rust coloured twinset which matched the skirt, her pearls and brogues. The dogs scratched at the garden door, June went to open it and let them in. They shook their old damp coats and settled themselves in their baskets by the log fire, and June went on writing letters.

Nanny said they would go on the same walk she used to take them always, down the drive and by the farm so that Charlotte could see the cows. Charlotte loves cows and calls them moo-moos like Roz used to. "Moo-moo was your first word, darling." Nanny brushed Charlotte's hair and said it was curlier than any of the Franklins' had been at that age; curly, fluffy, blonde it was. But her eyes were like April's, really blue and with thick lashes. She was a bit like April when all was said and done.

"April was never as fat as that, was she?" said Roz from the window seat without turning round.

June wrote to Dawson that everything was very strange here and that she could not believe that they would soon be on their way. She told him that the children were being very good on the whole and that Mademoiselle was quite cheerful. She gave him news about people in the neighbourhood and whether or not they were staying in the neighbourhood. She said that the Robsons had got an Anderson Shelter and that the Philipses had dug up their lawn already for potatoes, that the rector had finally left to be an army chaplain last Wednesday. She told him that they would probably bring more than twelve pieces of luggage in the end, and that she

55

had written to Pru's school to give them final notice. She wrote about bills she had paid and how much money she had left.

In the nursery Nanny stood Charlotte on the green linoleum. Charlotte stumped a few steps and then fell down and roared with pain and anger. Roz stayed looking out of the window. Nanny picked up Charlotte who was still roaring and rubbed the small fat hands. "Who sweeps the nursery floor these days, I ask myself?" She held Charlotte close and kissed her. "Precious angel, who is Nanny's treasure, then?"

June at the bureau looked across the lawn. She told Dawson that Nanny had come to lunch and to say goodbye and that it was Sunday and that the flag was flying and that she hoped his flag was flying also. And she told him that Alice Stephenson would have the dogs until they knew if they could be sent on a ship to Gibraltar or not, depending on magnetic mines.

This time next week there would be no-one left here in this house. Except Hudson the gardener who would look in each day. The cook, Mrs Colley, was going to spend the war in Plymouth with her married daughter, Mavis the housemaid had already gone to work in a munitions factory and the parlour maid was joining up to be a Wren. Hudson had flat feet and might not be called up at all.

Roz looked at the flagstaff and the frosted grass and said she didn't feel like walking anywhere.

With Dawson's letter, June enclosed Sandy's last letter from school. She did not enclose Pru's last letter because in this Pru announced that she had decided that she would not be confirmed and had stopped going to Confirmation Classes. If Dawson read that, he would simply say what nonsense and would make Pru be confirmed at once. He wouldn't listen to Pru's argument which was all about dogma, rationality, irrationality, useless ritual and not liking to wear white dresses. No point, thought June, in spoiling the reunion with argument. There was woodsmoke in the drawing-room, the dogs shifted in their baskets and June folded her letter, put it with Sandy's in the envelope and closed the flap.

Nanny, fastening Charlotte's coat, said Roz was just a lazy-

56

bones and always used to love a walk. There were better walks here, she said, than anywhere round Petersfield where she and Charlotte live with Nanny's sister. Charlotte loves a walk and Nanny takes her out for hours because the house is small and Nanny's sister's husband gets grumpy if they're in all day. It isn't easy with such a bag of mischief in a little house.

June took the letter out again: "P.S. you left some silk ties on your trouser press. You may not want them, but I'll bring them just in case. We all send lots of love. P.P.S. The dogs are well. P.P.S. Just think, we may get there before this letter. xxxxx."

Charlotte staggered round the nursery table and bumped her head and roared again. Nanny leant back in the chair and said that Charlotte would be the death of her. "This'll be the last treasure I take on, I tell you, Roz and April." She poked the coke stove in the nursery grate and said there was a chill in the room there never used to be in her time.

When they did set off for the walk, Roz watched them from the window, Charlotte with one hand held by Nanny and one hand held by April, going down the drive, but very slowly.

If you went on down the drive and through the farmyard, past the church and on across a field, you came in the end to the muddy beach, and from here you could look across to Thorney Island, which is called an island but is really a peninsula. There wasn't much on Thorney Island, but it was rumoured at this time that it was camouflaged to look like Portsmouth. The idea was that the Germans would bomb that instead of Portsmouth with its dockyards, barracks, shops and population. Bombs aimed at Thorney Island could fall wide, who knows, and land this side of the estuary on mud flat, field or church or farmyard, anywhere.

They went on down the drive, Nanny in her long grey coat and April in her Tam o' Shanter with her plaits bobbing as she walked and Charlotte staggering between them.

Roz stared straight across the lawn and hayfield towards the lane beyond and wondered how soon Mademoiselle would come back.

THREE

TAKE APRIL'S ATLAS which she won as the geography prize at the end of term and open it at the page which says Central Europe. On the left is the map of Germany, Austria, Czechoslovakia and Switzerland, with a bit of the top of Italy showing, and on the right, the map of Poland, Hungary, Rumania and the western part of Russia. Study the left hand page which shows that Germany, coloured brown, is dotted with towns and cities, like Berlin, Essen, Dresden, Frankfurt. And, in between the cities and towns there must be stretches of country, villages, hills and woods which are too small to be shown.

But we have road maps in England which we use when we are driving somewhere and these show smaller places. And there must be maps like that of Germany too, and people must look at them when they are driving somewhere. They have families too in Germany and they drive or go on trains and the mother or father will look out of the window and say look Heidi or look Heinrich at that church, that pretty farmhouse or that interesting pond. Look at those cows and see what different colours they are. Count the colours of the cows. Or do they play I Spy in Germany or I Love my Love in German? And do they have Swiss Mademoiselles but call them Fraulein and do they give them Sundays off and do the children wait for Sunday evening?

Beyond the lawn, beyond the hayfield and moving down the lane, a pinpoint of light if you strained your eyes to follow it. Then, where there was a hedge, it disappeared and would not be seen again until it turned the corner and came this way up the drive. Mademoiselle's bicycle lamp, blacked out with just a narrow slot to let the light fall on the way in front of her, appearing and disappearing, wobbling because the

58

drive is potholed, but getting bigger.

You had to stand with the blackout curtain wrapped behind you. The door of the night nursery had to be shut so that no landing light could shine outside. Mademoiselle rode up to the house in darkness on Sunday nights. The Air Raid Warden used to say on his inspections: "This house should be invisible." A kind of unseen house and, if all blackout was completely black and people had no torches, they could walk or bicycle all over England, bumping into houses, doors and walls.

The bicycle went past the house, along the drive. You could hear her after she had passed, opening the barn door to put the bike away, and shutting it again. Then you heard her coming downstairs, heard her speak to Mrs Colley, heard her going to the drawing-room, heard her coming up. Her crêpe soles squeaked on the linoleum as she reached the landing. And you waited. Sometimes she came in and sometimes not, when her crêpe soles went straight up the attic stairs.

If she did come in, it meant the day with Mr Brooxbank and the Meeting had been fun. Those days she came with Cadbury's chocolate which is made by Quakers (so is Rowntree's) and sat on Roz's or April's bed and ate as well.

The night of the Sunday Nanny and Charlotte came to lunch and tea, Mademoiselle came home early. She went into the drawing-room and the door was shut. All you could hear then were voices distantly.

Most Sundays she only went in there to say that she was back all right and to ask if everything was all right here and only spend a bit of time down there. And you opened the door on to the landing as soon as you heard her come in and waited only half in bed.

On good days she would play, would throw Sir Henry round the room and make him talk or sing or dance like Fred Astaire. She could do handstands on the floor, headstands on the bed; she could hold the two of you on either side of her to make a human pyramid.

This Sunday you were standing on the landing, very cold,

59

and leaning by the banisters, not hearing anything, no words, but only rising, falling voices, smelling woodsmoke which had seeped out round the drawing-room door. From Mrs Colley's wireless in the kitchen there was music, someone singing, then Big Ben, the news.

And going back to bed and not lying down but getting up again, on to the landing, cold feet, cold hands, woodsmoke in the nose and back to bed again.

Her days with Mr Brooxbank always started at Meeting. Sometimes the Meeting was worth talking about and sometimes it was what she called "not special", which meant that no-one had said anything at it. After the Meeting, and especially in the summer or on fine Sundays in the winter, Mademoiselle and Mr Brooxbank bicycled out of Portsmouth up on to the Portsdown Hills and had a picnic which Mademoiselle made before going and carried in her bicycle basket. Her bicycle, which she brought with her from Switzerland is a bright, light red and where it is not red, it's white; its tyres are white. It has the white cross on red background, the flag of Switzerland, in silk, which flies upon her handlebars.

One Sunday at midsummer she came home and Roz and April had not gone to bed. She found them on the lawn; they did their human pyramid for all the family and they did the acrobatic flight where the grown-up seizes the child by one leg and one arm and swings her round in swoops above the grass until you wonder whether it is the grass or you which is revolving at great speed, and have to catch your breath.

Once Mademoiselle and Mr Brooxbank cycled thirty miles to the New Forest. But usually it was the Portsdown Hills where, as they bicycled, they sang or yodelled, which Mr Brooxbank had learnt to do from Mademoiselle.

She met him first at Meeting soon after she arrived in England. "He is a friend," she said.

"A Quaker friend or a real friend?"

"Absolutely both," she said.

People they passed on roads and lanes as they bicycled

along singing and yodelling and so on and so forth, stared at them, Mademoiselle and Mr Brooxbank sometimes riding two abreast and holding hands, but only when there was no car or lorry or charabanc in sight.

"How old is Mr Brooxbank?"

"It is rude to ask."

She took a photograph of him; he was standing, wearing shorts and holding on to the handlebars of his bicycle by a five-barred gate. He wore glasses but was otherwise quite handsome, but he looked quite old. "How old do you *think* he is?"

"I do not think about such things. I only know he is a good man."

Mr Brooxbank had not always been a Quaker. He came to be one, Mademoiselle said, because he was absolutely fed up with all the other churches. Everything else he thought was all pretend, pretend singing, pretend kneeling, pretend crossing yourself. It was much better, he decided, just to think about God as Quakers do.

"When you want to turn into a Quaker, do you have to be christened all over again?"

'No. You just go to Meeting."

"And then you are a Quaker? *Tout de suite*?"

"*C'est ça*. That is the case."

For bicycling in the summer Mademoiselle wore a navy blue divided skirt and white aertex shirt with a blue badge on it she had for running in the team at University.

"Does Mr Brooxbank like Fred Astaire as well?"

"Oh yes, he likes him terribly."

Mr Brooxbank went to University once too, but did not do athletics. He was a teacher once but stopped teaching when he was ill. Then he started working as a carpenter in a furniture factory in Portsmouth.

The first bad Sunday happened in July; she came home when it was still light but went straight up the attic stairs. The bedroom door was locked and she whispered that no-one whatsoever could come in. For two days she stayed in her room and said that she was ill, only letting people in to bring

61

her food. Nor did she eat much food when it was brought to her.

Mr Brooxbank lived in Cosham which is on the edge of Portsmouth. He had not lived there long. "Where did he live before?"

"Somewhere else."

"Don't you know?"

"It's not important, but it was Southampton probably."

"Why did he move to Cosham?"

"Because he wanted to."

The Sunday after the first bad Sunday, Mademoiselle and Mr Brooxbank went on the bicycle ride and picnic as usual and chose the seaside, a small harbour and a beach where Mr Brooxbank had a swim. Mademoiselle could not say exactly where it was, but there were sailing boats and Mr Brooxbank said he would like one day to have a sailing boat, but they hired a rowing boat and rowed for hours and hours, taking turns with the oars and sometimes sharing them. It was so calm and blue that when they were a few hundred yards from shore, they rested on their oars and just looked at the sea and the way the sun was setting, making the sea all pink as far as the horizon. They laughed a lot as well and sang a bit as usual. Mr Brooxbank makes good jokes but Mademoiselle cannot usually remember them by Sunday evening. But after Sundays she would often sing a lot, songs like 'Just the Way you Look Tonight'.

Every year she was supposed to go home to Switzerland on holiday, but this year she did not go, partly because it seemed the war might start and she might not be able to get back to England. Instead she went on holiday to Cornwall to Mr Brooxbank, to where his sister lived. She bought two new check cotton frocks, one blue, one red, some new sandals and a bathing suit. It was beautiful weather there and Mr Brooxbank's sister was very kind, but unfortunately Mr Brooxbank was not very well while they were there and had to stay indoors: "What was the matter with him?"

"I told you; he was ill."

"Did he have a cold or flu?"

"No. Nothing special." It did not absolutely spoil the holiday and Mademoiselle went on a charabanc trip to Land's End and St Ives and bought everyone presents of blue and white china mugs and ornaments.

"Did he have a temperature?"

"It was not taken."

"Doesn't his sister have a thermometer?"

"I don't know, Rozzie, I don't know."

She sang less and there was another bad Sunday just after the holiday, the same Sunday that the war broke out. It broke out at eleven in the morning. It was difficult to know whether it was because of Mr Brooxbank or because of the war and *les sales boches* or because she was really ill that Mademoiselle stayed in her room for three days of that week. When meals on trays were carried up to her, she said, "Take it away. Keep it. We shall all soon be starving."

She did not go to Portsmouth after that for weeks and weeks. No human pyramids or acrobatics, but she made the children run several times a day as fast as they could from attic down to cellar carrying their gas masks and called it Air Raid practice, timing them to see who broke the record. She gave them French lessons after they came back from school and for days on end would not hear English spoken. They learnt the *Marseillaise* by heart and the only English song she would allow was one of Fred Astaire's, 'We joined the Navy to see the sea'.

And every now and then she went upstairs and stayed there, even on her birthday on the 31st October. They saved her presents but pushed cards under her door. You had to understand she did not hate you. You had to think about that hard to understand it.

At that time someone had to walk out in the garden every night all round the house to see if the blackout was complete. Turns were taken to do this, and one night when it was still autumn and not cold, Mademoiselle stood in the garden and shouted up at the sky: "Come on *les sales boches* and bomb! Buck up! *On vous attend.*" She ran around the house at least three times and stood well back from it across the lawn.

"Quakers are such good people," Roz's mother used to say. "I always believe Quakers are good people."

"Then why aren't we all Quakers?"

"I don't know, darling. I honestly don't know. I sometimes wonder."

"Mademoiselle says that, if everyone were Quakers, there wouldn't have been a war."

"I think I'd rather miss the dear old C. of E."

"But Quakers can't be soldiers or sailors, so Daddy couldn't be an Admiral."

"No, I suppose he couldn't, now I come to think of it." Mademoiselle always said that, if there were a war, Mr Brooxbank, because of being a Quaker, would go to be a stretcher bearer. But the war had been going on for quite three months and he was still in Cosham, still working at his job in the furniture factory and Mademoiselle went out again on Sundays. The frosty Sunday when Nanny and Charlotte came, she went off almost as soon as it was light, pedalling the red bike, muffled in her grey top coat, her white socks pulled up as far as they would go.

She came back and the drawing-room door was shut.

Voices, wireless music, woodsmoke. Words: "Gibraltar". More words: "Children", "Roz". Sentences or parts of sentences. June: "I feel for you most awfully ..." and, "Of course you must." Mademoiselle: "If only it was the case ..." and, "Never any of my own ..."

Wait on the half landing by the big arched window half hidden in the blackout curtain. Sandy's striped pyjamas come down over your feet, your hands are in the pockets of your dressing gown. They will be sorry if they find you here quite frozen. You have your watch with luminous hands and second hand. And that is Swiss. You have to plan what you will do when she does come upstairs at last. Decide to stay there on the floor as if you just happened to be there, but make sure she will see you. Don't look at her as she turns the corner to come upstairs and go on listening.

Or try to go on listening. Sit crossed legged. Hear the murmurs, hear the wireless in the kitchen go back to music and wonder what you'll do if Mrs Colley comes up first. Sit absolutely straight and still like Sandy does when practising his will power. They do it in the dormitory at school, he says, to see who can sit like that longest. He's never won and nor has Budgett. It's like Red Indians sit, he says. Red Indians, Sandy says, can sit for hours like that. Red Indians have a lot of will power.

It's like in church when you are waiting for the sermon to end. You count the seconds on your watch with luminous hands. But in church you have the prayer book and you can do things like learn the creed or work out from pages at the front the day which Easter will happen on in any year you choose. Or say the Our Father to yourself and say it faster, then faster still, and then backwards which is difficult at first. But listen for the drawing-room door.

They must have done it quietly. Silently. The footsteps coming up are coming quickly. Stay looking forwards, but then see that Mademoiselle has gone on up and reached the landing and has crossed the landing and is going up the attic stairs.

You never saw her face at all that night. She never even stopped; she must have seen you. She might at least have said "Hallo". People are supposed to say hallo to people. People always should say something to other people. Not speaking to people is one of the things it's rude to do. Nanny used to say: "I'm not at home to Mrs Rude." She could at least have stopped and said hallo or even told you to go back to bed. She should at least have said Go Back to Bed.

Silence the next morning while she handed Roz and April satchels, gas masks, sorting out their tangled leather shoulder straps. Silence, but not staying in her room so much, silence around the house, not even sighing. Neither *triste* nor *colère*.

She was starting to pack the trunks, folding clothes, sorting out summer things. She collected things from all over the house, carried them in piles and sometimes stood very still looking out of windows.

There are theories why she did not marry Mr Brooxbank:

Pru's theory: "Obviously he's already married. You learn more about married people falling in love with other people as you get older, falling in love with people they are not married to, I mean."

Sandy's theory: "He's probably half German or all German but got naturalised and took an English name. She found that out."

April's theory: "He thinks that if he married Mademoiselle, we would be sad because she'd leave. She would be sad too. So he doesn't want to make anyone unhappy by marrying her."

Another theory of Pru's: "He could be off his head, of course, but it only shows sometimes."

June: "That's entirely private to Mademoiselle. She hasn't done anything wrong. She is being very good about it. She is a brick and she's coming with us."

One day there was this man walking along by the field fence up the drive with a macintosh and carrying an umbrella. Roz came up behind him on her bicycle and slowed down to his walking pace, letting the front wheel wobble to keep her balance. He said he wanted to see Miss Taille, which is Mademoiselle's real name.

"I'll find her if you like."

He said he would wait and waited leaning against the fence. Roz went inside and her mother said: "Who's that leaning against the fence?"

"A man for Mademoiselle."

"Oh dear. I don't think she'll see him." June stood at the garden door with her spectacles on. "It might be Mr Brooxbank. I don't think she'll see him."

"It can't be Mr Brooxbank," said Mademoiselle standing holding a pile of clothes and not looking out of the window.

"Why can't it be?"

"Because he's gone away."

"He might have come back suddenly."

"Tell him I'm not here."

But the man was gone and was nowhere in the drive or lane nor by the bus stop on the main road. If it was Mr Brooxbank you would have thought he would have come by bicycle.

"Has Mr Brooxbank gone to be a stretcher bearer?"

"No, they will not let him."

"Who will not let him?"

"M.Y.O.B."

But if it was Mr Brooxbank in the drive, he was very tall, and the only thing against him being a stretcher bearer, you would have thought, was that the man carrying the other end of the stretcher would have to be as tall as him, or the wounded person on the stretcher would have his head higher than his feet or his feet higher than his head, unless Mr Brooxbank bent his knees.

Whoever it was had gone from by the field fence. He could have gone on down towards the church, the cemetery and the sea or across the fields to Emsworth or along the coast footpath east. Or anywhere. They looked for him, but not for long, and it got dark. There was a shadowy figure by the bus stop on the main road but it was not the same tall man.

She was singing and stopped singing. She talked and stopped talking, suddenly. She ran collecting things for packing, bouncing on her crêpe soles.

In Paris there was a wide street, and at the end of it, with the sun on it, the Arc de Triomphe. A band was playing. Somewhere there was the Eiffel Tower which they stood under and looked up at. Mademoiselle said she had once been up to the first storey of it, but was too frightened to go any higher. She said that when you walked up you saw, between the open iron work of the steps, the ground far down below, and it felt as if there was nothing between you and Paris far below but air. Everyone else said that they would go all the way up to the top if the Tower were open to visitors today. Mademoiselle said that she did not think they would and she would bet them that they would not.

They did some shopping in a department store before they started walking round Paris to see what their mother called the sights. They all bought things for francs. Roz bought four French model lead soldiers with bicycles; the soldiers being bent in a bicycling position with their hands slotted to fit over the handlebars. They had kit bags on their backs and rifles sticking in the air. Mademoiselle bought a pair of sun glasses because of the heat there would be in Gibraltar.

After shopping they walked very fast everywhere because their mother said that she had always heard that that was the best way to see Paris. Mademoiselle held Roz's hand and pulled her along until, when Roz could hardly walk, the others went on ahead to walk out and across into the Place de la Concorde, which was huge and surrounded with white buildings. Mademoiselle took Roz to a café where Mademoiselle had a *café noir* and Roz a *citron pressé*, which is both sweet and sour and a very good idea. "*Rien comme ça en Angleterre, Rozzie, hein?*"

"*Non. Rien comme ça.*"

They sat under a blue and white striped umbrella which had St Raphael written on it, which is the name of a drink and not a church, but also the name of a saint as well. Mademoiselle said that after the war she might come and work in Paris if it was still standing and had not been smashed to smithereens.

"Won't you come back to England with us?"

"I might. And if your mother wants me."

It was like summer. Roz took off her coat and jersey and sat in her aertex shirt, the sun hot on her back and shining into Mademoiselle's eyes across the round white metal table, so brightly that she had to put the new sunglasses on.

"I expect she'll go on wanting you."

"You think so?"

The umbrella was one of several umbrellas which were arranged in a circle round the square outside the café. When she had finished her *citron pressé*, Roz walked round and stood for a short time under each umbrella. Because it was late afternoon and winter, the sun was low; it came under the umbrellas and did not beat down on them, so they made no shade. When she came back to sit down again, she said: "After the war might be a very long time."

It was difficult to see Mademoiselle's eyes behind the sunglasses. Roz picked up her coat and got the soldiers out of the pocket and put them on the table. The sun made shadows of the spiky silhouettes on the white enamel. "You might *want* to come back to England ..."

"What for?"

"To see ... to ... see people, I suppose." If you pushed the bicycle along with the soldiers sitting on them, the wheels just turned; the soldiers wobbled but they just stayed on.

"What people?"

"No-one in particular." She pushed two soldiers on bicycles into the middle of the circle of the table, made them divide and wheeled them to the edge. "Anyway we might stay in Gibraltar for years and years."

"If we ever get there. Come on now. *Dépêchez-vous.*"

They said they would meet the others back at the hotel, where they were going to have the high tea the hotel would lay on for them especially. Mademoiselle walked fast again, pulling Roz in the sun across the Place de la Concorde and into a park called Les Tuileries.

"Why shouldn't we get to Gibraltar, Mademoiselle?"

"Oh *you* will get there."

"Why not you?"

"It doesn't matter if I get there."

They went on through the park along paths and came into the shade, so had to stop while Roz put her Shetland jersey on again and then her coat as the sun went completely behind the trees. "What will you do then? Jump out of the train?"

"Don't be silly, Rozzie."

"I only asked."

"Assez. Assez."

They went back to the hotel because there would be no

lights after dark in Paris, and Mademoiselle said just before they got there, "You see, Rozzie, it is the case that sometimes it does not matter whether I am dead or am alive."

Roz stopped beside a round stone pond where there must once have been a fountain in the middle, but which was now just a statue of two fish leaping in the air with holes where their mouths were but no water gushing out. "When *does* it matter," she asked slowly, "and when *doesn't* it matter whether you are alive or dead?"

Mademoiselle grabbed her hand and dragged her on: "We won't ever talk about it, you understand? I don't want to talk about it. I don't ever want to talk about it. *Jamais. Jamais.*"

"Is it because ..."

Mademoiselle walked on, dropping Roz's hand. Roz stood still and waited, and after a few paces, Mademoiselle also stood still. Roz caught her up and held her hand again. "Is it because ..."

"Rozzie," Mademoiselle yelled, so that a French man walking in the opposite direction along the path between the trees, turned his head. "I'll leave you here, completely alone in Paris, if you ..."

"I didn't say because of anything. I never said because of what. You couldn't leave me here."

"I could. No fear. I could."

It was twilight in Les Tuileries, but up above there was a patch of blue sky and a streak of birds flying in what they probably meant to be a straight line, but the line wavered and became curved, first at one end and then at the other, as one bird went faster or slower than the others. It was a thin line, like you would draw in ink with narrow nib, and very high. You didn't expect birds flying over places as big as Paris. They might have been flying east towards Germany for all anybody knew.

April brought her atlas with her; it's in her carrier bag, packed ready to be taken to the Gare d'Austerlitz. Look at the map of Central Europe once again. The birds might fly all night and get to Berlin in the morning.

In England in the last war, it is said, people hated the Germans even more than they do in this one. That was when names like Battenburg were too German and had to be changed to Mountbatten, and when the Royal Family changed from Saxe Coburg to Windsor. Nowadays people hate their enemies less, which is said to be much more sensible.

Mr Brooxbank may not have hated the Germans as much as Mademoiselle, so perhaps they argued about things like that. Perhaps he said *"sales boches"* as one of his jokes and she did not laugh and he was upset. Or perhaps Sandy is right with his theory that Mr Brooxbank is half German. Perhaps Brooxbank was once Brooxburg. Perhaps Henry, which is Mr Brooxbank's christian name was really Heinrich.

Not that he looked German standing by the fence and walking up the drive. He had on a felt hat so that you could not see the colour of his hair. Some Germans are fair with blue eyes, and some, like Hitler, dark with brown eyes probably. German children are usually blonde and wear uniforms, white shirts and sashes across their chests. The girls wear uniform too and march to bands. Mr Brooxbank did not look as if he could march to a band or would like to do so much. Although he was a bit like Fred Astaire, a bit, he didn't look as if he would be good at dancing. He looked rather tired and cold as he leant against the fence.

Theory: That they did not want him to be a stretcher bearer because they guessed he might be half or a quarter German and might pick up wounded Germans on battlefields as well as wounded English.

He was smoking a cigarette and wearing, not walking shoes which would have been right for a December afternoon, but sandals, the same sandals as he wore when Mademoiselle took his photograph.

Theory against last theory: No-one would really mind if he picked up wounded Germans because, as said before,

71

people are much more sensible about their enemies now, particularly the wounded ones. And the Red Cross has made rules about how enemies are to treat each other, so that war will be more fair.

Third theory: He could, by acting as a stretcher bearer, go further into enemy lines than ordinary soldiers and be a spy, or kind of spy. But, if they thought he really wanted to be a spy, they would not let him stay in Portsmouth near important dockyards.

April's theory: They could not let him be a stretcher bearer if he was half or a quarter or even an eighth German because he might tip English people off stretchers. And, if he is not a fraction German, they did not let him be a stretcher bearer because of some reason which is secret and curiosity killed the cat M.Y.O.B.

Letters may be forwarded to Gibraltar unless the war gets really bad, so Mademoiselle may hear from him again one day so you would have thought that it would matter if she got there. And if she really wanted to die, she would not have bought a *café noir*; she would not eat or drink at all. If she really wanted to die she could have thrown herself under a taxi in the Paris blackout. Or she might do it in the bath like Admiral Stephenson did, turned on the cold tap and then cut his veins apparently.

FOUR

DAWSON CALLED TELEGRAMS wires and he sent one
from Gibraltar: LOVE TO ALL BOTH LARGE AND SMALL STOP
PUT YOUR FAITH IN GOD AND THOMAS COOK.

He was always sending wires; he sent bets on horses to his
bookie all his life in coded wires. He ordered things from
shops by wire and sent complaints by wire when the things
he ordered did not come at once. He complained by wire to
the B.B.C. when they did not pronounce words properly and
complained by wire to manufacturers when their goods were
faulty: 16 H.P. MORRIS CAR COMPLETE WASHOUT, he wired
Lord Nuffield once.

June sent wires too: LOVE FROM ALL BOTH LARGE AND SMALL
STOP WE PRAY TO GOD AND TRUST IN THOMAS COOK STOP ETA
LA LINEA 23 DECEMBER 1800 HOURS.

La Linea is on the Spanish Gibraltar border and they will
arrive there by car four days from now. The barrier, white
painted, will be lifted and the Admiral's car will be on the
other side. And to get there they will leave Gare d'Austerlitz
in Paris at 20.50 hours on the 19th of December.

June strides along the platform with her bag strap on her
shoulder and the same tweed coat and skirt and brogues and
twinset, having had a lovely day in Paris considering it is war
time and mid winter. They have seen the Eiffel Tower, the
Arc de Triomphe, walked down the Champs Elysées and
seen the outside of the Louvre and bought things at the
Galeries Lafayette. Like a mild autumn day in Hampshire,
it was, this day in Paris.

June walks towards the central hall. It's much the same
as any railway station as far as she is concerned, a lot of
shunting noises, steam and swirling luggage trolleys. A lot of
soldiers, sailors, kit bags, people standing, waiting, people

73

kissing, shaking hands. French people do shake hands a lot.

It was a lovely day in Paris; the journey's going better than she expected and the hitch about the sleepers on the train can only possibly be temporary and Mademoiselle will soon arrive with all the luggage.

Her children stand on platform 12, the train above them, waiting to get on it. This train says WAGONS LIT in yellow on blue background. It has brass rails which lead up to the corridor. The *Wagon Lit* Attendant stands at the bottom of the steps. He holds a clipboard and a pen and has a list of passengers. The Franklin names were missing from his list and so the children wait.

June said, before she left them on the platform. "There must be a mistake. *Il faut qu'il y a une bêtise.*"

Pru said: "Honestly Mummy—not *une bêtise*—that means something like a sin. It's not the *Wagon Lit* Attendant's fault. He can't help it if our names aren't on his list."

Pru leans against a station lamp. Above the lamp, the roof of the station is somewhere up there in the steamy darkness. Pru leans against the lamp; her arms are folded; she has taken off her coat and stands in the yellow polo-neck sweater which she bought today and dark green kilt in which, like Roz and April, she travels all the time. This evening Pru wears silk stockings and high-heeled sandals. Last night at the hotel she tore up an old vest to make curling rags and her pageboy style is still there, still bending slightly, swinging on her shoulders. She leans against the lamp post with arms folded, sometimes looking down at the *Wagon Lit* Attendant and sometimes looking down at her silk stockings and her sandals and the way the pleats of her kilt just reach her knees.

The *Wagon Lit* Attendant, when he is not checking names of passengers on his clipboard, looks at Pru.

April sits on an empty luggage trolley, with her paper carrier bag beside her. What April bought today was a rubber doll with painted dark brown curly hair and very dark brown eyes. He looks a little like the *Wagon Lit* Attendant.

74

Steam hovers in a halo round the lamp post where Pru stands. She watches pass between her and the long French train a stream of people, French civilians, soldiers, sailors, moving, and some of these go up the steps and into *Voiture* 60 waved there by the *Wagon Lit* Attendant.

Roz on the luggage trolley next to April kicks and swings her feet in dark green socks and leather button shoes. The model soldiers and their bicycles are in the pockets of her coat.

The stream of people passing them thins out. The *Wagon Lit* Attendant calls to Pru: *"Ça va, hein?"*

And Pru calls back: *"Non. Ça ne va pas. Nous n'avons pas de lits dans la voiture soixante."*

"Ah! Dommage!"

"Oui, c'est ça!" says Pru.

Sandy bought a Morse code set in Galerie Lafayette. He stands with it under his arm a little way from the luggage trolley and in the shadows well away from the lamp post on which Pru is leaning. Sandy in the shadows in his dark grey coat and long grey flannel trousers, while on the trolley Roz's feet still swing and April takes out of the carrier bag her English rubber doll and says it is a twin to the new French one.

"Anglais?" says the *Wagon Lit* Attendant, calling Pru again.

"Oui."

He gesticulates with his clipboard towards her kilt. *"Ou peut-être Écossaise?"*

"Un peu," says Pru.

He laughs. *"Les jambes sont Écossaise's et la tête Anglaise?"*

"Non. Pas du tout. Pas comme ça."

Sandy's Morse code set is in a square cardboard box wrapped up in brown paper tied with string. Inside are two Morse code tappers and two buzzers, two transmitters, two receivers and a battery. April says she's calling the new doll Paul after the Prime Minister of France, Paul Reynaud. Her English doll is Marietta.

"Notre grand-mère était Écossaise."

"*Votre bonne-maman? Et voilà! Moi aussi. Ma bonne-maman était Écossaise.*"

April has a twin tucked under either arm; they match the symmetry of her plaits. Roz says you cannot have twins who are one French, one English. April says they are adopted twins, so there. She has not been sick at all in Paris but has left her Tam o' Shanter somewhere.

Pru shakes her hair and folds her arms and saunters towards Sandy and as she moves her shadow grows, her legs are even longer. On the platform opposite there is a hiss of steam, doors banging, carriages begin to move, soldiers, sailors running for them, swinging on the doors and shutting them. The train on platform 13 leaves. And Sandy says to Pru: "What did the *Wagon Lit* Attendant say?"

"He said his grandmother was Scottish."

Their mother runs towards them. She is distinguishable by her run as well as by her face which is pale and by her hat which is in her hand, not on her head, her jacket flapping open. Her hair blows back. She runs like she runs in mothers' races at school sports or as she runs after Pru's pony in the paddock when it does not want to be caught. She pants at the bottom of the steps of *voiture* 60. The children stand close by but she pushes them aside. "*Monsieur, je ne pouvais pas trouver l'homme de* Thomas Cook. *Il faut que vous nous donner des lits.*"

"*Il n'y en a pas, Madame.*"

"It's no good, Mummy. He's shown me. They've all got other names on."

"*Tous occupés. Tous occupés.* All occupied. None are free. *Comprenez?*"

"I understand French quite well, thank you."

"He's only trying to help you by speaking English, Mummy."

"But I have tickets. *Billets.*" She waves them near his face.

"*Ça ne fait rien,*" the *Wagon Lit* Attendant shrugs his shoulders.

"*Les Billets. Regardez. Je les ai achetés de l'office de* Thomas Cook at Portsmouth, *Angleterre.*"

76

"He really can speak English quite well."

"Be quiet, Pru."

"We leave soon. *On part bientôt*," says the *Wagon Lit* Attendant.

"Vous ne pouvez pas. Nos valises ne sont pas arrivées."

Sandy moves away. He faces Platform 13 which is empty now. In the train which moved away from there arms waved and windows were pulled up, blinds fixed.

The *Wagon Lit* Attendant puts two hands on the brass rail and hoists himself up the steps, two at a time. Doors further down the platform slam. He stands at the top of the steps and turns, looks down.

June calls up to him: *"Vous ne pouvez pas quitter cette gare ici avant que nos valises sont arrivées. Vous ne pouvez pas. Je vous demande très sérieusement; je vous en prie; ne quittez pas. Nous sommes une famille anglaise qui vont chez,* I mean *à,* Gibraltar, *et il faut que nous arriver là-bas avant de Pâques,* I mean *Noël. La père,* I mean *le père, de ces enfants ici, il est une bonne amie, un bon ami des tous les gens français, je vous assure, Monsieur ..."*

Pru walks away, arms folded, and stands beside the lamp post once again. Roz and April stand below the *voiture.* Holding the brass rail, you can feel the vibration of the slamming doors, the bump of luggage in compartments. June has one foot on the bottom step, one spare hand on the rail, her face upturned.

And Mademoiselle is sitting beside the taxi driver, leaning forward, peering through the blackout as they speed towards the Gare d'Austerlitz. Because in some *Arrondissement* or other, they had a puncture; not far from La Bastille, she thinks it was; there was a bump, the taxi stopped, brakes squealing, and there in complete darkness, she waited while he changed the wheel. She leant against a wall below a window; people inside were eating dinner; you could hear their voices and the sound of plates. Outside she heard the driver crank the wheel jack; she heard it slip, she heard him swear. She thought she might be spending Christmas there and all the war, and thought of the *sales boches* breaking through the Maginot line, crossing France with tanks and armoured cars, and into Paris, goose-stepping up the Champs Elysées. And wondered if the people inside that house would still be eating dinner in the evenings then. It seemed like hours and hours before she could get into the taxi again, and then they drove at even greater speed across the Pont d'Austerlitz.

"*Mon mari,*" June's voice carries, even over people's running footsteps and the station tannoy which echoes with a new announcement in the roof. "*Mon mari, le père de ces enfants ici, sont,* no sorry, *est, un amiral dans les marines anglais. Il défend à* Gibraltar *tous les bateaux, les navires, qui passent entre la Méditerranée et dans l'Atlantique. Il est un officier très important. Voici mon passeport. Le regardez. Voici nos billets de* Thomas Cook. *Avant la gare,* I mean *la guerre, mon mari a visité en France avec le roi d'Angleterre, et il parlait avec votre Président et votre ...*"

The children move to the empty luggage trolley and sit down. Sandy puts the Morse code box on his knee, Pru folds her arms and looks up at the station roof, April sits with a twin on either side of her. Roz takes two of the French soldiers out of one pocket and two bicycles out of the other and balances them on the trolley. Their mother's voice carries towards them. "*Il faut absolument, absolument il faut ... les pauvres enfants ... mes enfants ... s'il vous plaît.*" They look neither at her nor at each other.

Mademoiselle runs silently towards them, faster and with a more economic use of limbs and energy than June. Her white blouse collar flashes in the station lamps; behind her the mountain of Franklin luggage comes up out of the dark, pushed by one porter with another scurrying beside it to make sure the pieces of it do not fall off. Trunks at the bottom, suitcases and holdalls thrown on top, sliding, bumping as the trolley stops.

A voice above them in the station roof. "*Départ de quai douze ...*"

The *Wagon Lit* Attendant is inside the train, in the blue-lit corridor.

"... *de quai douze* ... Bordeaux, Bayonne, St Jean de Luz, Hendaye."

June shouts: "Get up children! Get in the other end." And to Mademoiselle: "You help me. It's no good talking to them." The children run the length of *voiture* 60 and climb up the further steps. Inside they see the *Wagon Lit* Attendant.

June on the platform taking suitcases, carrying them up the steps. Likewise the porters and Mademoiselle. Inside, the *Wagon Lit* Attendant looks first wildly towards the children at one end then at the luggage coming in the other end. *"Non, non,"* he cries. *"Pas possible."* He reaches up to the top of a window in the corridor, unfastens it and slides it down. And shouts.

June on the steps pushing holdalls, trunks, which Mademoiselle and the porters carry up.

Passing by, another porter hears the *Wagon Lit* Attendant's shout. He stops and stands. He grabs the empty luggage trolley, the one the Franklin children sat on earlier. He wheels it to the window. A Franklin suitcase is heaved out by the *Wagon Lit* Attendant. Another follows it, a trunk, and then a holdall and another trunk. There is another pile of luggage on the platform, growing all the time.

"... Bordeaux, Biarritz, Bayonne, St Jean de Luz, Hendaye."

June's high voice echoes after this. "Stop him children. Stop the *Wagon Lit* Attendant. Stop him doing that!" Her face in the blue light is a screaming mask. Then she can be seen back on the platform by the growing pile of luggage. She grabs a piece from it, carries it back to the steps again. June, shouting to the *Wagon Lit* Attendant that they do not want his sleepers, that they only want to travel on this train, that they will travel anyhow; they have the tickets, he can't stop them; they are English, British travellers travelling to English, British territory. Her voice is hoarse through shouting. She took off the jacket of her coat and skirt and flung it with her camel coat to Pru along the corridor.

Mademoiselle in her white blouse is on the platform, hands
79

on hips, Pru is in the corridor in her yellow sweater, Sandy, Roz and April one above the other standing on the steps, and June comes down quite slowly past them. She stands between the porters on the platform in her twinset, strand of pearls and navy blue tweed skirt. Behind her go some sailors with white hats, red pompoms on them.

More doors slam down the platform.

"... Biarritz, Bayonne, St Jean de Luz, Hendaye."

A small man coming up the platform; he wears a stiff round *képi*, has braid on the jacket of his uniform and a whistle on a white lanyard hanging across his chest. He walks outside the Hendaye train towards the Franklins. June turns that way and watches him come steadily towards her. She stares at him, but is not seeing him.

La Linea lies on the flat end of Gibraltar just this side of the Gibraltar race-course, if you are coming there from Spain. It is approached on either side by flat white roads, and the frontier post itself is painted bright white. Beside it is a low wooden building painted navy blue and fenced with posts and strong white rope. The grass verge of the road, once you enter British territory, is watered and mown and the grass edges chopped off neatly. The Franklins will approach it from Seville, driven in the naval car which will have met them there, and Dawson will approach it from the official residence high up on the Rock, driven there in his own car by a naval driver, an Admiral's flag in silk flying on the bonnet. The doors of the two cars will open and the white-painted frontier barriers will be raised. There will be shouted orders and the stamping of the boots of the ratings as they are brought to attention and to salute. There will be shouts of children, and Dawson, when he has saluted and received salutes, will hold his arms wide open.

At least that was how it seemed it would be in four days' time, ETA LA LINEA 1800 HOURS DECEMBER 23. June stands in the Gare d'Austerlitz by *voiture* 60 of the train, arms folded, waiting for the man in cap and lanyard to come up to her, ready for him, expecting him to bring some kind of verdict that the barrier, white-painted, at La Linea will be raised in

80

four days' time and no car from Seville will be on the far side and no greeting.

The children also wait and watch her.

What a wild goose chase, people said before she left, what an awfully daring thing to do my dear, I do admire you. And now Dawson would say she was all adrift, all goosey, all haywire. And Nanny would say she had known all along that it would end in tears.

THOMAS COOK COMPLETE WASHOUT she could wire to Dawson.

It is *too* bad. It really *is* too bad. Worse luck, as the children would say, hard lines and rotten. How awfully, terribly disappointing and a raw deal at that, pipped at the post at the eleventh hour and by a pipsqueak of a *Wagon Lit* Attendant. June stands under the lamp post Pru leant on earlier and hears Pru's voice carrying above all the racket and all the noise of doors and steam and other voices: "Well *do* something. Can't we all just go? Don't give in just like that for heaven's sake. Honestly. We've got to *go*."

NO ETA LA LINEA STOP NO ETA AT ALL STOP NO GO. OH DAWSON I AM SORRY.

Something about the cardigan of her twinset draped around her shoulders gives her the appearance of defeat, as the man in uniform comes nearer.

She touches her strand of pearls and waits.

Real pearls, not false, not *ersatz*, not synthetic. Not even cultured pearls which are made by encouraging the oyster to produce, by putting in its mouth a piece of grit to irritate it. Real pearls like June's are those which oysters make spontaneously.

A rich godmother laid down a pearl a year for June. When June was twenty there were twenty pearls and for her twenty-first birthday present, the necklace was completed. Tiny, carefully graded, increasing in size from the catch at the back of her neck towards the centre of the necklace where it hangs on June's breastbone, bobbing as she moves on cashmere wool of jersey. Small, delicate pearls, which, when the threading breaks, can only be repaired by a London jeweller in Pall Mall and must be sent there in a strong small cardboard box by registered post.

She has another strand of pearls for wearing when her real ones are at the jewellers. But these are cultured; the difference is unnoticeable to everyone but her.

She touches them again. She is on the train. In the first class restaurant car at a table where a pink shaded lamp throws light, its tassels moving with the train. A man sits opposite, the King's Messenger, in black jacket and wide silk tie; he lifts his brandy glass.

She wears her naval brooch, a crown set on royal blue enamel, but no other jewellery except her pearls, her gold watch and her wedding ring. Most of her jewellery is in the safe of Barclays Bank in Portsmouth.

There will be dinner parties on the Rock at which she will preside, the Admiral's wife and younger than you might expect because of the age gap between her and Dawson. But never mind; it works, his wisdom, wit, experience, her youth and gaiety, fair skin and energy, have carried dinner parties in the past when she could wear jewellery, earrings, rings, but never bracelets.

In another world June went upstairs at half past six to change for dinner, opened her jewellery case and decided what to wear tonight. In such a world she had a lot of evening clothes, silver shoes, gold sandals, floor length skirts and lacy blouses, silk stoles or fur stoles for the winter.

The godmother who gave her pearls now lives in Bournemouth in a huge old house with lots of servants too old to be called up, luckily. June looks at the King's Messenger and touches her pearls again.

He came up on the platform following the guard. This man in a bowler hat came up out of the dark, and in the lamplight could be seen to wear a bowler hat, a black coat and to be carrying an umbrella. He raised his hat to June.

A clean pale face beneath the bowler hat, a greyish white moustache. Behind him on the platform came a porter, carrying in either hand a strong white canvas bag. The diplomatic bag. Two diplomatic bags.

He raised his hat. He was the slightest bit familiar, perhaps the kind of figure who might once have been seen or still might just be seen going along the Mall in London or going under Admiralty Arch or crossing Trafalgar Square or walking up Whitehall.

He offered help; he was the kind of man you might see in the *Daily Telegraph* with Mr Chamberlain, walking behind, a tall and slightly stooping man. He raised his hat and offered help. He spoke to the *Wagon Lit* Attendant, to the guard and all the porters. He put his hat back on his head and climbed inside the *voiture*, bending slightly through the door.

And June was saying things like: "I don't know what to say," and, "You really can't give up your sleeper," and, "I wouldn't dream of it."

But looking back she knew her darkest hour was over. What a blessing and what a brick and what an awfully nice man the King's Messenger turned out to be.

A first class sleeper has a bunk made up with navy blue blankets and clean white sheets. There is another bunk in case you want another passenger in there. There is a lav as well beyond another door, and a basin and a mirror where the King's Messenger, if he slept in here, would have shaved tomorrow morning.

The Franklin luggage is piled from floor to ceiling; the diplomatic bags have gone. The King's Messenger found another sleeper, having spoken for a longish time to the *Wagon Lit* Attendant. He also found seats for Sandy, Pru and Mademoiselle a long way back along the train. In the first class sleeper June will have the bottom bunk and April and Roz will share the extra one above.

First stop will be Bordeaux in the middle of the night, then through Biarritz and out again while it is still dark, and on towards St Jean de Luz and Bayonne to Hendaye just after dawn. They lie with April's head by Roz's toes and Roz's head by April's toes and Mademoiselle is there to say goodnight to them.

She says she did not know if she would catch the train at all. It was so dark in that *Arrondissement* that she could not see her watch to tell what time it was. It was *affreux* and absolutely ghastly, and it made her very timid in that dark street where there seemed to be no-one walking at that time of night.

In the first class sleeper she tells the children: "Get into the bunk now, *tout de suite*, both of you."

While the man was exchanging the tyre she kept telling him all the same to be extremely quick and to buck up about it. But he was dense and a bit gaga and it was altogether *épouvantable*. Completely awful in fact.

"Rozzie, you have the end by the window, but *ne touchez pas les* blinds, and April, you go that end where it will be warmer." There was a point, says Mademoiselle, waiting in the street while the driver mended the puncture saying a great many swear words she had never heard before, and she believed she would be spending Christmas and all the war in Paris with sixteen pieces of luggage and only a few francs. Great Scot, she says, good heavens and *quelle horrible* experience to have gone under, and Roz and April sit up facing each other in the top bunk with the luggage swaying on the floor beside them.

"When you wake up, you will be in Spain," she said. "They say '*olé*' in Spain." They asked her if she liked the Spanish people and she said they were Okay probably but Franco was a friend of Hitler's which made him quite impossible.

She kisses them goodnight and seems to mean it. She seems to be quite glad she got to Gare d'Austerlitz in the end, and they lie rocking with the movement of the train as Mademoiselle slides the door shut and goes to her seat a long way back along the train.

King's Messengers carry messages from the Foreign Office to British Embassies in capitals of other countries. People who become King's Messengers, Pru says, were usually something else before. They probably were naval officers or in the army, and left because they knew they would not get promoted any higher. This is sometimes called being retired early. This King's Messenger is fairly old but when he took his hat off he had quite nice thick grey hair and was not bald at all.

It must be quite nice being a King's Messenger, having your ticket bought by the Foreign Office and a first class sleeper definitely booked.

This King's Messenger is travelling not to Madrid or anywhere in Spain, but to Lisbon which is the capital of Portugal which is like Switzerland, like Sweden and like Ireland, another neutral country.

FIVE

JUNE SITS IN the short-sleeved jersey of her twinset with the cardigan thrown over the chair-back. Beside her, and inside the fixed, drawn blinds of the first class restaurant car, there are pink crushed velvet curtains bound with silk and fringed. The King's Messenger raises his glass of brandy. *"Bon voyage."*

"Oh yes, of course, *bon voyage*." She lifts her champagne glass. "And thank you once again."

The pink light from the lamp fixed to the table reflects on the rosewood panels of the carriage walls. Waiters walk, carrying silver plated trays of cheese and silver coffee pots along the centre aisle. The King's Messenger had a bottle of champagne with dinner and June has only joined him for a drink.

Delightful, charming, knowledgeable, urbane are words she might just use for him. He's probably ex-army; the cufflinks on his stiff white shirt have on them what might be a regimental badge. He has a pallor which suggests a time in India. June sips champagne.

He does this journey often, knows the waiters by their names, the hazards of the frontier crossing and the intricacies of the Spanish Civil War, now over luckily. "It was tricky travelling then."

"I'm sure it must have been," June says.

They have talked of this and that, of rationing at home, of gas masks and the A.R.P.; she has told him who she is and where she's going and he has told her that this restaurant car may be running for the last time on this train.

June loves champagne: "This is a treat, you know. It really is. A spree, like peace time."

"Yes."

86

She was right. He is ex-army and has been in India. They talk of Mr Chamberlain, Lord Halifax and other members of the Government. June loves champagne or any kind of sparkling wine and could drink them all until the cows come home.

"The last champagne?" she asks.

"Well, possibly, alas," he says.

The King's Messenger has a wife called Mildred and an only son called Alastair. He talks about the Spanish Civil War again: "You'll see the devastation."

"How terrible," says June, and asks him if Alastair has been evacuated anywhere.

The champagne bottle moves in its ice-filled silver bucket and the handles ot the bucket are hinged rings set in the mouths of silver lions and tap against the bucket with the movement of the train. The King's Messenger tells June that his son Alastair is spending the war in Scotland with his grandparents.

"How nice. What part of Scotland?"

"Perthshire."

"I have some cousins there," says June.

The fringes of the pink silk lampshade swing and the train rocks as it gathers speed well south of Paris now. Across the aisle sit four French army officers. The King's Messenger talks about Mildred now and how she misses Alastair. "She misses him most frightfully."

"I rather dread the journey across Spain," says June.

"I should take some drinking water with you."

"Oh yes, of course. What a good idea."

Across the aisle the four French army officers lean over bowls of soup. Above their heads their hard round caps are hung on hooks and bumping with the train. They drink their soup with table napkins tucked into the collars of their uniforms. And the King's Messenger says Mildred, because she misses Alastair so much, is thinking of taking up some war work.

"How very sensible," says June. "A very good idea."

He fills her champagne glass from the bottle in the bucket

and puts the bottle back. Mildred, he says, has always been a restless person.

"I expect you've moved around a lot," says June. "I often think that army people do."

The King's Messenger and Mildred were in India, then in Singapore and then came back to England, but Mildred isn't fond of England and has never settled very well. She hated Aldershot and Camberley and was miserable on Salisbury Plain. They live in London now.

"I'm rather fond of Salisbury Plain," says June.

The French army officers take chunks of bread and soak up the remains of soup from soup bowls; they eat the bread and lean back in their chairs and wipe their mouths on table napkins. June watches the King's Messenger, touches her pearls, and, as she lifts her hand, the gold chain of her wrist watch flashes in the lamplight.

"In fact," the King's Messenger says, "she has been rather nervy ever since the show began."

"The show?"

"The war."

"I see," says June. "Oh yes."

"It's hard on women, I can see."

"Well I suppose it's hard on everyone."

"I see you are one of the carry-on-regardless school of thought."

June stares at him. "I honestly don't know. I never really thought about it. Dawson and I ..." She looks at the French officers again, she sips champagne and wonders how the little ones have settled in the sleeper.

"Perhaps it's because Alastair is her only one."

"It *is* sad for only children, I always think," says June.

"We married late."

June puts down her glass and sees the bubbles rising.

"So, you see, she couldn't ..."

"Oh I'm *sure* she couldn't ..." Only children are to June sad children in stories who look out of windows.

"She had a frightful time with Alastair ..."

"I'm *sure* she did ..." Only children go on their own to parks with Nannies.

"Another would have killed her ..."

"I'm sure it would ..."

The French officers have plates with steak on them. When they raise their eyes it is towards each other and they talk in low voices.

"Alastair is a fine fellow though."

"I'm sure he is. He must be."

The King's Messenger lights a cigar and the smoke curls into the lampshade and rises parallel with the rosewood panelling of the wall. Mildred, it seems, is delicate, and to June she sounds a little *difficile* as well; it must be a worry for the King's Messenger that she is alone in London in the war.

"Of course she has a lot of friends."

"Of course she must do." June gazes into the distance at the far end of the restaurant car where waiters come with food on trays from kitchens. Mildred sounds vivacious in a way but perhaps not awfully good with children and animals or fond of gardening. "When you were in Aldershot," she says, "did you know the Wesley-Smiths?"

The French officers have finished eating steak and now have vegetables on their plates, eating them separately as most French people do. Champagne tingles the nose; you can feel the bubbles before you taste them. Beyond the door through which the waiters come is the tunnel which connects the restaurant car to other carriages forward in the train, and beyond that somewhere is *voiture* 60.

April, when she is trying to go to sleep, moves her head from side to side on the pillow, and when she has gone to bed with her plaits done up and their ends still in rubber bands, these plaits shoot up and down and whip on the pillow as her head rolls from side to side. It is said that, when she was a baby, she started doing this, shaking the bassinet against the night nursery wall so that it could be heard from the next room and even from downstairs.

Roz, at the window end of the top bunk, puts a finger to the blind and pulls it back and sees out there darkness in which white flashes of steam blow past, but there are not lights on anywhere. She has a torch shaped like a fountain pen which Sandy swapped with Budgett last term at school and which he lent her for the journey. It gives a pin-point of light which travels round the carriage, landing in turn on the swaying pile of luggage, on their coats hung on the door into the lavatory.

June stares down the restaurant car and hears the King's Messenger telling how he and Mildred always went on holiday abroad before the war, to Italy or to Greece and how Mildred misses that sort of thing.

"Do you think Italy will come into the war?" asks June.

The pinpoint of light is a tiny circle on the ceiling of the carriage above the bunk, and the bunk itself rocks with the train and the train itself moves faster all the time and is going along past trees and houses with people in them, and both the houses and the trains have blinds or shutters drawn, and no-one in the houses knows about the bunk and Roz and April on it, and Roz and April do not know about the people in the houses, and April is asleep in any case.

The King's Messenger says that it is hard to say if Italy will come into the war or not.

"No, absolutely," says June. "And how can anyone tell when all is said and done?" and she asks him if, when he and Mildred lived on Salisbury Plain, they came across a Peter and Freda Le Mesurier who've always lived in Wiltshire.

This train, this *voiture*, this top bunk of the first class sleeper, of which the people in darkened houses the far side of the blowing steam are unaware. At home it is the same but opposite because home is only a mile from the main road and a mile and a half from the railway line where people are on trains all night to Portsmouth or to Waterloo, passing the house and having no idea at all of the Franklins and the other people living with them and all the animals inside. Blacked out house with pieces of square material, curtain rings sewn round the edge by Mademoiselle and April, hooks screwed into the window frames to which the curtain rings are fixed. Blacked out house and blacked out train.

A silence in the restaurant car because the rails are smooth. No rattle from the champagne bottle, nearly empty though it is, and only the King's Messenger goes on talking: "We think," he says, "that Alastair will be safe in Scotland."

"Oh surely yes," June frowns. "Oh surely yes. Why ever not?"

The four French army officers are drinking wine.

"We look at it this way," the King's Messenger goes on.

The four French army officers turn and listen, and the King's Messenger swirls his brandy in his glass: "We think," he says, "that by the time that anything happened in Scotland, the balloon would have gone up everywhere ..."

June stares at him.

"One can't help thinking ..."

June sips a nearly empty glass.

Even the church at evensong was blacked out, but not very well, so they had to use candles to sing the *Magnificat* and the *Nunc Dimittis* and the vicar made the sermon short and the hymns were from the section of the hymnbook called For Times of Trouble, Famine, Pestilence and Disaster.

And in the restaurant car the King's Messenger leans back and says how he and Mildred, like Mr Churchill, could see it coming and had always thought that Scotland would be best for Alastair.

And April now asleep lies flat on her back, her hands folded across her chest and looks like the statue of the crusader's wife in the side aisle of the church at home. White stone, that statue is, and smooth and cold; it might be alabaster.

"Mind you," the King's Messenger leans back, "I found this time in London a degree of pessimism I hardly had expected."

"Oh no! You didn't! Oh, it's wicked to be pessimistic. Dawson and I ..."

91

"Defeatism even." The King's Messenger looks up at her.

The pinpoint torchlight points straight up and makes a circle on the ceiling the size of a sixpence, or, held closer to the ceiling it makes the size of a silver threepenny bit. Further back it widens to a shilling. Then switch it off and on again.

"I ought to be going really." June drains her glass.

"The worst instance of defeatism this time," the King's Messenger says, "came oddly enough from some friends of ours in Felixstowe ..."

June stares at him. The French officers have had cheese brought to them. She grabs her cardigan from the chairback.

"This chap, this friend of ours, is a medico, a surgeon ..."

June sits upright and puts her cardigan on, jerkily. Her eyes are shining from champagne and in the lamplight. "I think defeatism," she says, "I think defeatism, pessimism ... I think that sort of thing is very wrong ... I think people who talk like that ... I think they should not talk like that ... I think."

And switch the torchlight on and off, make Morse code on the ceiling. Morse code all the alphabet and then again, for practice. And then the Lord's Prayer slowly forwards and then backwards as the train gets noisier and rattles through a station.

The French officers are eating cheese, scooping Camembert from a china dish and spreading chunks of it on bread.

"This chap, this friend of ours—he would call himself a realist rather than a pessimist ..."

The champagne bottle, empty, rattles in the ice and bangs the bucket edge; June holds it steady, not looking at the King's Messenger any more, but down towards the tablecloth.

"He's got a family—like you—about the same ages as your bunch I'd say—and, should the worst occur ... and thank the Lord, by the way, that Mildred was out of the room when he was telling me ..."

June opens her mouth to tell him that she'd really rather

not hear all this, that she does not awfully like to hear this sort of thing, that ...

This train is going on. First stop Bordeaux and swaying rather more than it did before, so that waiters stagger in the restaurant car, and in the sleeper the torchlight flashes wildly on the ceiling.

"So his story is that he's laid in a stock of ... well ... of something pretty swift and efficacious ... and his story is that a good many of his friends have asked him if ..."

In *voiture* 60 on the ceiling, flash: And bread daily our day this us give heaven in is it as earth on done be will thy come kingdom thy name thy be hallowed heaven in art which father our.

They could be hurtling towards Bordeaux or they could be hurtling anywhere. June stands up. She checks, as she has come to check at every move she makes, that her money belt is still around her waist. She adjusts the sleeves of the cardigan at her wrist, she picks her shoulder bag off the chair. The King's Messenger also pushes back his chair. "Er ... well ..."

"Well thank you so much ... very kind ..."

He stands. "Well ... are you sure ... ?"

She says quickly, "Oh yes ... absolutely ..."

"Well ... I hope ..."

"It's very kind of you ..."

"I just hope everything ... your journey ..."

"Of course it will be ... perfectly ..."

She sways through corridors and needs to stop and grope for her spectacles from her bag to read the numbers of each carriage as she goes.

Sandy, when he was a little boy and teased by Pru, would block his ears, put his hands over his ears and say: "I am not hearing you. I simply am not hearing you."

It's cold out here as if a window or a door was open somewhere to the night. It was not true of course. The King's Messenger might have made it up. Or his friend in Felixstowe might have made it up.

Here is a window open, half way between the restaurant

93

car and *voiture* 60, and the blind flaps in and out of it.

Surely, surely, surely it was not true. Surely if people felt that pessimistic they would send their children to America.

She stands in the dark sleeper in the tiny space between the piled up luggage and the bunks. Level with her head lie Roz and April, a pair of feet and a head at each end of the bunk. The only light is from Roz's torch left on. June picks it up, switches it off and puts it on the lower bunk.

Surely people wouldn't; no-one did that in the last war, no-one ever did that in a war, not in England. Or the Empire anywhere.

The only thing to do is to go to bed or go to bunk. Half-dressed to go to bunk. Take off the skirt but keep the twinset on, the money belt, the stockings.

Perhaps not everyone of course can send their children to America.

Even like this, it's cold. June gets up, goes round the luggage and unhooks her camel hair coat from the door.

People do not do that sort of thing. And, if they do, they do not tell people that they do it. Casualty lists in papers are enough, and air raid shelters are enough, and gas masks, seeing children in them, is enough.

Cold as she is she sits up and puts her hands together palm to palm.

The extraordinary thing about the Spanish Civil War, the King's Messenger said earlier, was the way the two sides were raring to get at each other. Fervour, he said, was the word for it. Fervour. People wanting to fight each other. People being absolutely certain they were on the right side.

"But everyone *is* sure they're on the right side, aren't they?" June said.

"Oh yes, of course ... but taking a broad view historically, dispassionately ..."

"Of *course* we must be on the right side," June said.

He told her a story about the Spanish Civil War, about how the Nationalist forces were besieged in Toledo, in the Alcazar, and how, when they had eaten all the dogs and

94

horses except one, they groomed the last remaining horse, which was a pedigree, a racehorse of great power and speed. They did not eat this horse but kept and fed and groomed it as if it were about to run at Ascot or the Epsom Downs.

Her eyes are closed. But that was Spain and Spaniards.

In England, after all, the theatres have re-opened and in the *Daily Telegraph* which Sandy bought she read that Princess Elizabeth and Princess Margaret-Rose have come back from Scotland to be with the King and Queen for Christmas.

Cold in the first class sleeper even with blankets and coat drawn up under her chin. Psalm 23 again is what she says tonight.

Several minutes ago the train stopped and people could be heard outside and, when she pulled the blind away from the window, there were torches moving and French voices. Although they must have moved some way south by now, the compartment is colder than ever. Roz and April were well covered so June took one of her blankets and slid the door of the compartment open.

Six carriages down, she counted earlier, and it is easier to walk there while the train stands still, but she walks on tiptoe.

There is a jolt, the train moves once and twice and each jolt carries it forward with a clank as carriages bump together. June clutches at the rail which runs along the corridor and enters, with the train still jolting, the dark deserted restaurant car. Another jolt and she is thrown against the edge of the table where the French officers sat earlier. The torch in her pocket bumps against the table and against her thigh and the train begins to move more smoothly out of whatever station in the night this was.

Five empty corridors down the train and only in a few compartments are there lights, and in these, soldiers, sailors lean with empty bottles on the floor and with their windows steamed with breath and smoke from cigarettes. Here, in the sixth corridor, no lights are on, but there is a smell of cigarettes, of garlic and cheap scent. As the action of the train becomes smooth and fast, you turn the corner into this carriage and count compartments as you go along the corridor. At the fifth, take the handle of the door and prepare to slide it back.

It is dark inside and only shapes of figures to be seen. Take Roz's torch from pocket, switch it on, but no light comes. People around you shift in seats and the air is cold and musty. Stand back to let what light there is from the corridor fall on the faces of those within and whisper: "Sandy?"

He is in the corner nearest, back to the engine. Someone must have swapped places with him to let him have the corner seat, but it is difficult to see where his coat ends and the next person's coat begins. It is only possible to see that he is smaller than his next door neighbour and that his head lies on that neighbour's shoulder. June lifts the blanket she carried folded on one arm, and holds it up in the doorway of the carriage, unfolds it until it is a double thickness and leans with it towards Sandy. Someone moves at the far end of the compartment and a match is struck. Other heads jerk up, including Sandy's, and his eyes open. The light of the match shows his eyes wide open, but dark eyes under a high white forehead with no fringe, very dark eyes, not Sandy's, staring at her.

June stood back, slid the door shut quickly. She's in the dark dim corridor again and will have to try again. The next compartment or the one before or the one after that or the one before that. Sandy's thirteen now, and, should the war go on for five years ... well, we take that in our stride. If we are bombed we're bombed. If we are mined ...

96

SIX

SAY TO YOURSELF as you walk towards this bridge
across this river, say "France, France, France". And when
you are on the bridge say "No man's land, No man's land,
No man's land". And as you reach the other side, the barrier
and the soldiers, say "Spain, Spain, Spain". Walking behind
the trolley, which is more like a red rusty wheelbarrow and
unlike any other luggage trolley seen before, pace the steps,
examine the colour of the stones beneath your feet and
observe the difference between the stones of France and the
stones of Spain. Then march on, following the trolley as if
it were the gun carriage at the King's funeral or the gilded
coach at the Coronation with the King waving out of one
side and the Queen out of the other. Head held up across
the frontier, even if one string handle of your carrier bag
is missing and you have to hold it, arms around it, and walk
on.

"This is Hendaye," Pru said before they set off towards the
bridge. She pronounced it "Awndye". "These mountains,"
said Pru, holding out her arm and turning full circle to
indicate the mountains, "these mountains are called the
Pyrenees. Look. There are villages on the lower slopes. These
villages here are in France and those villages there in Spain.
Over there is Irun. That is the Spanish border town and this
is the French side of the border. This is Hendaye."

April was sick while they were waiting still in France outside the passport control shed. She leant down with her head
between the red holdall and the green trunk before Pru could
reach for the beach bucket which sat up on the high-piled
smaller cases, its red handle an arc against the clear early
morning mountain sky.

June and Mademoiselle were in passport control and had

been there since just after the train arrived. After April had been sick everyone said it was either the cold which had made her sick or perhaps the altitude. Pru and Sandy lifted the trunk and the holdall away from the spot where April had been sick, then Pru went on describing the scenery they were looking at: "It is unlike the Alps; they are not so green on the lower slopes as are the Pyrenees. These mountains all around us here are the Pyrenees."

"But you have never seen the Alps," said Sandy.

"The air is like wine," said Pru, "isn't it? And the sky the most incredible blue we have ever seen. This is Hendaye and on the far side of the bridge is Spain, is Irun. These are the Pyrenees."

Sandy stood with his hands in the pockets of his overcoat looking over what was still probably France, although a bit further on where the bridge began it would be No Man's Land where there was barbed wire. In the last war there was barbed wire; one of his uncles had been killed by a shell while caught on it. Many people's uncles died like that. Or were gassed, like Budgett's father who was gassed, but died much later, after Budgett was born, but still because of gas.

Behind Sandy, the train they had come on backed out of Hendaye Station to the North, shunting, sending up steam between the mountains and opened up further the view of the surrounding Pyrenees. In the distance to the south there was a Spanish station and a Spanish train which would take them to San Sebastian.

Pru stood behind him. "Wouldn't it be odd," she said, "if there were frontiers like this in England, say between Hampshire and Surrey, so that to get from, say, Aldershot to Farnborough you would have to go through passport control?"

"But you wouldn't," Sandy said. "Aldershot and Farnborough are both in Hampshire."

"They are not. Aldershot is in Hampshire and Farnborough is in Surrey."

"Budgett lives in Farnborough and his address is Hampshire; it's on the school address list."

"You are completely wrong, you know. Farnborough has always been in Surrey."

April and Roz stood between the piles of luggage, their heads invisible, but they could see the tops of the mountains above them in their triangle of sunlight beyond the shadow cast by the passport control shed. April, because she left her Tam o' Shanter in Paris somewhere, was bareheaded, and the air, which Pru compared to wine just now, had stung her ears, but the complexion of her face showed no change from its consistent pallor. It was still to be compared to the alabaster of the crusader's lady's statue in the church at home.

Step out from between the piles of luggage still in the triangle of sunlight. That must be east because the sun is low and makes you shield your eyes. It rises there, and there must be the sea.

Turn round and face the west and see your shadow starting from your feet. And this is west. And, if you stood just here all day the sun would come up behind you and would stay high until it was tea time when it went behind the mountains.

Ten yards away Pru said what nonsense it was to be arguing about Farnborough and Aldershot when they were all about to enter Spain which was a land of suffering at that time, and when they were high up in the Pyrenees, and when they might soon be within sight of Guernica where the worst atrocity of the Spanish Civil War took place, and in the country of the Basques who were a proud and independent race. What had Farnborough and Aldershot to do with those places where Louis Macneice and Ernest Hemingway came to observe and fight, and George Orwell also, and during which three years of bitter fighting ...

"You are only saying that," said Sandy, shielding his eyes with his hands from the low sun, "you are only saying that because you don't want to admit that you were wrong about Farnborough. And the Spanish Civil War started in July 1936 and finished this year, in April, actually, which makes it not three years; two years and nine months."

"Three years all but three months," said Pru.

They stood in the cold bright sun as the shadow it cast over the passport buildings shortened, and their own shadows across the platform towards the pile of luggage also shortened, Sandy in his thick black overcoat and Pru with her coat undone over the yellow sweater and the dark green kilt, her feet feeling the bite of the cold platform in her high-heeled sandals.

Twenty-five years later, Pru said: "At Irun we had that long cold wait and that silly argument about Farnborough and Aldershot."

"No. That was at Hendaye. Before we crossed the bridge. At Irun we had the argument about the dates of the Spanish Civil War."

"No that was at Hendaye. We saw the King's Messenger go off over the International Bridge. We were about to cross it too, to catch the train to San Sebastian; it was very beautiful, snow-peaked mountains all around and little villages perched on slopes and Spain in front of us ... And we came to San Sebastian that morning, and rightly has it been called the pearl of the Cantabrian Coast, set as it is in jewel-like setting along the sandiest beach in Europe. The summer capital of Spain has arisen like a Phoenix on the ashes of the older cities and now offers broad avenues of tamarisk and pine and palm. These trees stir lightly in the breeze and sails appear on the horizon and we ..."

In the middle of the afternoon June belted her camel hair coat over coat and skirt and tied the emerald green headscarf over her hair. She did this standing outside the swing doors of the hotel and set off along the pavement with Pru at her shoulder and Sandy a few steps behind. They walked fast towards the sea front past closed shops and shuttered windows, the wind lifting the point at the back of June's headscarf and Pru's hair from her shoulders. They walked, hands in pockets, heads ducked away from the wind off the sea and faces turned towards the buildings as they passed.

A stiff wind blew sand up from the beach which was the sandiest in Europe according to the Spanish guide book Pru had bought in Paris. A north wind, it must have been because the beach faces in that direction.

Pru wore for the first time on the journey her long school scarf, a purple scarf which streamed out behind her.

June said this seaside town reminded her somehow of Weymouth or maybe Eastbourne or Torquay and Pru said that by no stretch of the imagination could you be anywhere in England. *Everything* was different, absolutely everything. Sandy turned up the collar of his coat, stayed a few paces behind and said nothing.

The stone of the buildings which faced the sea across the road and promenade was very clean and there were tamarisk trees, bending with the wind across the pavement. June said that there were tamarisk trees in Cornwall. San Sebastian reminded her of Penzance. High above June, Pru and Sandy there were seagulls slipping sideways across the sky in patches of blue between fast clouds.

"Well, I think this is perfectly lovely," said June. "Perfectly lovely. Nice and clean and not spoilt by trippers."

"Trippers are what seaside towns are for," said Sandy, shouting from behind.

"I think it's lovely, don't you, Pru?" called June.

Pru did not answer. Between them and the sea was a wide road and the equally wide promenade, steely grey and shining with recent rain. The sea itself out there was a paler grey and the waves appeared higher than the esplanade itself.

Pru had left her guide book at the hotel but she was usually good at remembering things. She was fifteen at the time with her hair blown out of pageboy style.

They crossed the wide road towards the sea and stood on the front where the tamarisks were blown to bend towards the town. June said it was windy but mild like the west of Scotland often was when she went to stay with cousins there.

This inlet from the Bay of Biscay which is the Bahia de la Concha or Shell Bay in English, has in it the Island of Santa Clara which they looked out on as they stood beside a shelter on the promenade, which shelter *could* have been seen in Eastbourne or in Weymouth, Torquay or Penzance but would have looked extremely out of place there because the wrought-iron was curved in such elaborate curls on the back-to-back seats inside and the roof was decorated with curlicues. Although, as June pointed out, you do get curlicues on promenade shelters everywhere.

"Not curlicues like that," said Pru. "There's a great deal of eastern influence in Spanish architecture."

It was breezy, fresh and bracing, June said, walking on, hands in pockets, headscarf flapping, and Pru and Sandy followed, keeping up her pace but never quite catching up, faces turned towards the sea and then away from it.

"San Sebastian," Pru shouted to her mother, as they crossed the road to head towards the town again, "escaped serious damage in the Civil War. It was only bombarded from the sea."

"It's lovely," June shouted back, "lovely and old-fashioned and quite unspoilt."

They followed her across the road and went beside a park where there were more trees, not only tamarisk but pine and palm trees, the taller palm trees had their leaves tied in bunches. "Staked," said June, "against the wind. I'd never have believed it. The Spaniards must be quite good gardeners."

There was a square with shops and narrow streets leading off it. They walked unimpeded by other walkers in the afternoon because it was siesta time which, June said, was such a good idea for people in this sort of country.

"I wonder," Sandy said, "if they stopped fighting in siesta time in the Spanish Civil War."

The street enclosed them and the pavement here was narrow.

Pru at fifteen, five foot four, eight stone seven, knew more than anyone else in the family about the Spanish Civil War because her form mistress who was also her English teacher read them writings on the subject, and also had a brother who was in the International Brigade.

June strode in front along the narrow pavement. Here there were iron grills with sharp points in front of ground-floor windows. Spanish people, the few that were about, hurried along because perhaps they were missing their siestas. June

102

talked as she walked, but many of her words missed Pru and Sandy and were carried forward in the wind which followed them.

The church they came to along this street they came upon quite suddenly; it was set back with a small open square of reddish stones in front of it, but with a wide white front and bell-tower.

Pru was not keen on church, disliked religion, did not want to be confirmed, but her form mistress, Miss Bridges, said there was a lot of art in churches worth looking at and hoped Pru would see some of that in Spain.

In the small square the sun came out, dazzling them. June went to the steps up to the door and grabbed the round iron handle, rattling it. Her voice came back to them. "Churches in England are never locked."

"It doesn't matter," Pru called. "It's not a cathedral or anything; it wasn't even in the guide book—and it will be freezing cold inside."

June went on rattling and turning the circle of iron which was the door handle of the church until Sandy went to help her, took it in two hands, pulled the door towards him, turned the handle and pushed the door open slowly.

"Put your scarf over your head now, Pru."

Pru hesitated. Then she said, "Oh all right then," and draped the purple muffler loosely. Its ends hung down her coat on either side.

It was dark but not cold, a smell of dry warmth and candle-light from the altar end, and incense. June sniffed. "Of course ... incense." Her whisper was penetrating and filled the darkness. "Oh of course yes ... incense."

There were no pews such as you have in English churches but rows of chairs which filled half the cavernous space, and above was a high flat ceiling supported by smooth white pillars. They kept near the middle, skirting along from pillar to pillar. On their right was darkness which contained, per-haps, side chapels, tombs and unseen doors. June's carrying whisper became subdued, awed and full of wonder: "Oh I can't help thinking that it's very beautiful."

103

Sandy moved away from them and stood just behind the back row of chairs and about the dead centre of the church, facing the altar at the far end and seeing it as a blur of light and red and gold.

"*Typically* R.C. of course, but *very* beautiful," June whispered, walking up the aisle towards the glow and standing there, feet apart, chin up, centrally.

Pru some yards behind saw that there were candles lit on either side, a red glass lamp above and that all these illuminated a painting of the holy family.

"I suppose," June went on looking straight in front of her, "I suppose that it is more interesting than an altar cloth."

In the painting, Mary was holding Jesus up to some bright light. There were reds and blues and the light she held Him up to was glowing yellow. Pru walked towards the altar end, and, passing her mother, went up the altar steps to examine the painting more closely. She stood, leaning between the candles and tried to read the signature.

"Pru!"

"I'm only trying to see who painted it."

There was nothing more to see. Pru went into the shadows behind the pillars and saw her mother still staring up. There was that expression on her face which came over it when you told her something surprising or impressed her particularly or astonished her. You could see all that from the candle and the red lamp glow. Then you could see her look round into the darkness and hear her whisper. "Sandy, Pru, where are you?" and see her go back to looking at the painting.

Pru shook her head and let her scarf fall off her head on to her shoulders. She knew about religion being useful to people who needed it; Miss Bridges taught her that; Pru wants to be someone who doesn't need it.

Sandy walked from the middle of the church back towards the entrance where the door was still open, letting a rectangle of yellow sunlight on to the flagstone floor. This door was an immense door, oak, studded with iron bolts half an inch across, and the wood of the door itself must have been five

104

inches thick. Sandy put his hands on either side of it and swung the door slowly on its hinges until it was nearly shut, so that the rectangle of sunlit stones dwindled proportionately to the amount he moved the door. The weight of the door must have been a ton, but because it was supported down one of its sides by hinges, Sandy, weighing six stone ten pounds, could move it. Sandy was six stone ten when weighed at school by matron on the last day of this last Christmas term. But at the beginning of that term, in September, he weighed six stone nine, which meant that somewhere at school he lost a pound. His parents could have complained about that, sending a six stone ten pound boy back at the beginning of term and getting one home at Christmas who weighed only six stone nine.

Pru waited with him by the door while June came up the church towards them. Her expression was back to normal, unwondering. They would now be heading for the next place. Her normal voice returned, but outside the sun was beginning to go off the square, the wind had dropped, and across the street a light had been switched on behind one of the iron-grilled windows.

"I must say," June said, her voice echoing back against the white front of the church, "I must say Roman Catholic churches are very fine to look at in their way."

Pru and Sandy followed her along the street and back into the broad square where they felt the sea breeze again.

"I only came to see if there were any interesting pictures," Pru said.

"Well, it was quite a beautiful picture in its way."

"Not very important, though."

"Very important really, Pru, when you come to think about it."

"I mean not painted by someone important ... the church we should have gone to see ..."

"Oh I see. Honestly you children know so much about these things."

"Only what people ought to know."

It was half-light. They stood still on a paved place with

105

spaced tamarisks around them. There was a statue but they could not read its name. "I wish I'd brought my guide book with me," Pru said. Lights were coming on in shop windows along the avenue.

"I must say," said June, "I do think it rather a pity ..."

"What?" said Pru.

"Well, all this about not being confirmed."

"Well, it's definite."

"I think religion is such a help to people in life, you know."

"I know you do."

June walked away from the statue. The trees made the path a narrow avenue. Her hands were pushed into the pockets of her coat and her scarf re-knotted firmly under her chin. She stumped, almost. Sandy and Pru went on looking at the statue, which was of a Spanish general on a horse, and then realised that their mother had gone to the edge of the paved place and was heading back towards the hotel.

June walked away from them.

Pru: born after twelve excruciating hours of labour and being told to be brave and grit your teeth. But otherwise everything that could be asked for from a first child except that a boy would have been more welcome. Not much more though. Snapshots of Pru over June's bed at home are of a grinning baby and of a grinning toddler and of a grinning school girl with lengthening, thickening plaits. Pru: first prize for funny sayings as a small child, all recorded. First step, first word, first tricycle and first bicycle, first pony too, recorded, recollected. First beating from Dawson when she was aged eight for not practising the piano when ordered to. Second beating the next week for not practising the piano when ordered to. Third beating the following week. Six weeks later they let her give up the piano. School, day and boarding. Present school, such an awfully nice one full of awfully nice and interesting children from awfully nice and interesting families. Pru's friend Oenone's father is a don at Oxford. Pru's friend Clara's father is or was a Governor of the Leeward Islands. School uniform colours the same as the colours of the suffragette movement. You could not have a more modern-minded and delightful school. Pru's friend Sylvia's father is very high up in the British Museum and a baronet. Pru: awfully happy at all her schools, awfully naughty too of course. Pru writing to say she was not going to be confirmed. Awfully naughty, but probably she'll change her mind one day. Pru growing up, wanting bust bodices, which she calls brassieres, silk stockings and suspender belts. Pru doing what is known as making eyes at people. Not exactly pretty, but attractive, people say. Vivacious.

June grew up in baggy flowing dresses, was presented at court and became a debutante in the early twenties but was not a bright young thing.

She walked fast away from the avenue not bothering if the children were following her or not. Half shut your eyes, and, apart from the smell of something pungent coming from a basement in the street of San Sebastian, you might be home walking up the lane and heading for the house across the gravel and into the front door.

Pru saying she would marry who she wanted. June saying yes of course she would because that was what girls do nowadays. Pru saying that she might not marry at all but live in sin. June saying that would be rather disappointing really and that everyone found the right man after a time. Pru saying that she couldn't believe Dawson was really the right man for June because of all the times they quarrelled. June saying that of course married people quarrel. Pru answering that quarrels don't speak very well for good marriage, do they? June saying Pru will learn. Pru saying that she has nothing more to learn. June suffering and blinking away that recurring event of being reduced to tears of anger.

She, June, stayed in the nursery and the schoolroom until she was sixteen and grew up on that birthday and had her hair put up, in the middle of the last war, that was, and didn't know much at that time about the world, or men, or sexual intercourse. Pru knows it all of course and oh how lucky for her and oh how tiresome she can be about it.

June hurrying past smells of what is probably garlic and

between Spaniards fresh from their siestas back to the hotel on the sea front at San Sebastian, away from tiresome adolescent children who think they know. Sometimes she turns her shoulder to avoid a Spaniard, wondering if she has found the right street which will lead back to the sea front and the hotel.

June always tells Pru that she is very lucky to be brought up free and easily and not kept in the nursery or the school room. Pru points out that she is sent away to school which comes to the same thing. June says that going away to school makes people independent. All right, says Pru, well I am and that means I can choose about things like not being confirmed and getting married or not getting married. Anyway, she says, there is a girl at school who always does exactly what she wants and is not a virgin any more. June says she is sure that cannot be true. Pru gives evidence that what happened to this girl is true and that it was a soldier and happened on the day the war broke out and at a party. June points out that the first day of the war was a Sunday and people certainly would not have had parties. Pru said her mother had no idea how other people lived.

June kept going through the half dark streets. Sometimes she stopped people and said "Hotel De Londres y de Inglaterra?" but could not understand their directions. She could only follow the way they pointed.

Pru and Sandy took the street out of the avenue which passed the park and led on to the promenade again. You could only see the sea now where lights reflected on it, but you could hear it and could smell it. They half ran beside each other. Then they stopped beside the shelter which their mother had said might be in Eastbourne. Pru took off her scarf and let it blow horizontally in the wind. It blew out stiffly parallel to the ground and, when she turned full circle, the scarf stayed blowing north to south so then she had to twist her arm above her head as she had seen Spanish dancers do in films, and the scarf still streamed in the same direction from her hand. "I'd like to have some castanets," she called to Sandy.

They hurried on and might well be back at the hotel before their mother: "She might have easily lost us," Sandy said.

"Don't be silly; she'll get lost before we do."

"There's no point in arguing with her, I sometimes think."

"People can't learn things after a certain age."

"Crikey, what an awful thought."

Pru spent last night in a third class carriage between two French sailors and they slept with their heads on either of her shoulders. One had soft curly hair and one was bald. They smelt very slightly. Their knees touched against the silk stockings of her knees and she felt the side of their knee caps and knew how their knees would be hairy and bony as men's knees are. She sat with her own knees close together because if she crossed one leg over the other, the buckle of her sandal strap might catch on her stockings. The event of the two sailors was exciting enough to write to Oenone about, but after several hours it was too uncomfortable to find exciting and sleep was more important. Pru supposed that quite often being close to men was boring. She had not thought of that before.

At that time Pru had been kissed twice by a boy who she went riding with, and once by an older boy who knew how to kiss with the mouth open so that you found each other's tongues. She had also been kissed on the cheek by older and much more attractive men like Kay's Bernard. Her dreams were of being kissed, mouth open, by a man like Leslie Howard and putting her hand on the back of his neck where his hair grew to a point. She had also at that time had a man put his hand on her knee in a cinema when she went with the little ones to see *Snow White and the Seven Dwarfs* in Portsmouth. He had also taken her hand and put it on the outside of his trousers. This was as much as had happened to anyone in Pru's form at school, but not of course as much as had happened to the girl in the sixth form on the day war broke out.

When Pru walked under street lights in San Sebastian with Sandy, Spaniards turned their heads and said "Bella" to her. She was stunning in her stockings and sandals, kilt just swinging at the knee, and knew it, even if her tweed coat was childish and too short. She stopped worrying that her hair had blown quite straight again and let it stream out behind her with the scarf.

"This is the *paseo*," she called out to Sandy. "At this time of day in Spanish cities, people walk. They simply walk and walk. It's like a kind of party."

The greatest compliment ever paid to Pru took place three days ago. In Kay's flat, Bernard looked at Pru and said: "Don't you think, Kay, that she has bedroom eyes?"

There was also Miss Bridges who taught Pru English and about the Spanish Civil War. And, as often as Pru thinks of something about sex about which to write to Oenone, she thinks of something about Spain about which to write to Miss Bridges. Miss Bridges lives in Ipswich and spends the holidays with her widowed mother. It must be very boring for Miss Bridges, but it must be nice for Ipswich to have her there. Miss Bridges is lean and about twenty-nine years old. She has an Eton crop, but very well cut, olive skin and dull brown hair streaked with blonde from her summer holidays with another mistress at the school, in Greece. Another dream of Pru's is that she will somehow one holiday happen to be in Ipswich and will call upon Miss Bridges. Miss Bridges would give her tea at her mother's house, and afterwards they would walk across fields together and Miss Bridges would say, as she once nearly said, that Pru was one of the best pupils in English she had ever had. Pru was never quite sure what would happen after that.

"*Bella*" was called out eight times under the lights of the promenade at San Sebastian. And when you considered that this country had recently been devastated by the most terrible civil war in recent history, that was not bad.

They pushed through the swing doors of the Hotel de Londres y de Inglaterra and saw their mother disappearing up round the corner of the stairs.

In the train Pru woke up first. In the early morning, light

came into the compartment round the edge of the drawn blind and she crawled to the end of the bunk and let the blind up. What was outside and what the train was passing now were rows of grey-greenish bushes planted in rich brown earth. These must be olive groves and were not divided into fields by hedges. Olive groves of grey-green, no, grey-green-silverish plants stretching away on a wide flat plain which was somewhere in Spain between San Sebastian and Madrid. Pru took her writing pad out of her writing case and wrote at the top of the page: "Somewhere in Spain" and then the date, and then "Dear Miss Bridges ..."

In the compartment were two suitcases, hers and Sandy's, on the floor with clothes and spongebags jamming the lids open. Their coats, his black and her green tweed, swung on hooks beside the washbasin. She knelt up on the bottom bunk in her yellow sweater and green school knickers and faced the window, watching flicker past the grey-green-silverish olive groves on rich newly-turned brown earth, and beyond it she considered the colour of the plain the train went through and lifted her eyes to the range of snow-covered mountains which were beyond the plain, and decided that they, at any rate, were pink. A pink range of mountains, not even white at the bottom because you could not see the base of the mountains where they blurred into the uncoloured plain.

Somewhere in Spain.

Dear Miss Bridges,
    Here we have grey-green-silverish olive groves on rich newly-turned earth and beyond them a plain which has no colour and beyond that, mountains which are pink ...

Because it was cold in the compartment, Pru put on her stockings and suspender belt and strapped and buckled on her kilt and went on writing:
"Yesterday we saw San Sebastian ..."
By the time Sandy woke up, the view from the top bunk

111

was that of wet fields and roads and winter trees and it was raining. He lay, looking out, with the blankets still over him and his grey school shirt unbuttoned at the neck. He was thirsty because it was stuffy in the carriage. At school he slept with the sash windows of a high dormitory wide open. He looked at his watch and saw that there were two hours at least before they reached Madrid. But, before arriving in Madrid they would eat the food Mademoiselle had brought from the kitchens of the Hotel de Londres y de Inglaterra because there would be no restaurant car for breakfast on this train.

The food consisted of bread which is called black but is only brown and very hard and stale, no butter, a cooked chicken and some oranges. They had breakfast in one of three double sleepers, but not everyone ate any of it. April did not eat because she had been sick twice in the night, and Roz was sulking because she did not like any of it, crying most of the time and snivelling in between. Mademoiselle was upset because the picnic basket had been lost, probably off the trolley on the International Bridge, and the food from now on had to be wrapped in parcels.

Pru went back to finish her letter. There was an hour before Madrid. Sandy said he was still thirsty even though he had had an orange for breakfast. He kept opening the window and trying to catch rain in the palm of his hand and licking it. His eyes were half shut against smuts and raindrops. When his fringe was lifted by the moving air, up from his forehead, you could see where his skin was white and washed and where it was dirty with train smuts and grubby rain. They went through several small towns, and on their stations stood people in macintoshes waiting for suburban trains to take them to work. They were nearly in Madrid, but there were still stretches of muddy country in between the towns.

They'd had some Perrier water the night before, fizzy in bottles and pretty horrible, but most of this was drunk by April after being sick.

Huge buildings came into view on a hill outlined dark grey against a pale grey sky. There was something about

112

these buildings which made them seem incomplete; some of their windows were missing. Now, as the train passed underneath these buildings on their hill it was possible to see that all their windows were missing. Jagged stone edges instead of window frames. There were floors missing and the buildings were open to the sky.

There was not any coffee and there was not any tea. The thermos flask, which was in the picnic basket, was either pinched or fell in No Man's Land.

About this time, the train started to slow and another train over-took it, carrying commuters who stood in the corridor looking out at Sandy and Pru sitting in their compartment, with their coats on by that time, passing on another line. The rain was turning to sleet also at that time, because Madrid is on very high ground and liable to snow-falls in the winter.

They were coming into the Estacion del Norte which served, as its name suggests, lines approaching Madrid from the north. Sandy said that this made it something like King's Cross or Euston. Pru said that he was as bad as their mother, thinking of everything in English terms.

"It was going to be very cold getting out of the train and I rather wished I'd put on my school socks and walking shoes again. You could tell it would be cold from the way people huddled on the platforms.

"We got all our things into the corridor. Mummy had put her emerald green scarf on April and kept tying it tighter under April's chin. Then there began to be a fuss about Roz's carrier bag. She shut it in the door of her compartment, and the only remaining handle of it bust, broke through the paper, came away. Sir Henry Rabbit, her French soldiers, her pencils and paper and playing cards all fell on to the floor in the corridor. She made such a fuss about it that, in the end, Mademoiselle picked up all the things and stuffed them into April's carrier bag. Meanwhile the corridor was crowded and Sir Henry got stepped on by some Spanish people who apologised and were quite nice about it. But Roz went on snivelling and looking disgusting. I remember them (Mademoiselle and Mummy), I remember them saying to her that, because she had bust the handle of her carrier bag, she must now carry April's with all their things in it and that, if she bust the handle of this one, then she would probably lose not only Sir Henry and her French soldiers but all April's things as well and that she might well be left behind in Madrid. We probably said that it would be good riddance to bad rubbish because that was the sort of thing we used to say. Roz always said we were unfair to her because she was the youngest, but that was nonsense because there are a lot of advantages in being the youngest of a family. And there is no truth in the rumour that her birth was a disappointment and that she was a mistake. I think they had been hoping for another boy, but they always took even the biggest disappointments in their stride. Roz was always grumbling and wanting to be a boy. And she grumbled that morning that the carrier bag she had to carry was too heavy for her.

"There wasn't, in the end, room for Sir Henry Rabbit in the bag, so Mademoiselle made Roz take off her snake belt. It never kept her kilt up properly anyway; the kilt was always slipping down. Mademoiselle put the snake belt all round Roz outside her coat and round Sir Henry too. He was strapped to Roz.

"Then Mademoiselle used the pieces of Roz's carrier bag to wrap up the remains of the chicken in, and some bits of bread because she thought we might not get anything to eat in Madrid at all. She had some white string, tied and knotted it and made a parcel of the food. And shoved it under April's arm.

"April was shivering as she often did, even when she was not cold, and Roz was crying still. We always used to say that she would never be able to remember what things looked like in her childhood because most of the time the things she saw through tears. Sometimes she was known as the watercress bed and sometimes as the village pump and sometimes as the albatross because she was always round our necks.

"Anyway, when our train stopped, it turned out that we
114

were not, after all, facing the platform, but facing the other line where the commuter train was standing, sending up smoke and steam to blot out the windows of our train. So we had to move everything across the corridor tripping over each other, Mummy pushing and shoving as usual, Roz wailing, Mademoiselle sighing and April looking like a rather pathetic refugee with her little all in a paper parcel."

Pru: Allowed whole chapter. Fair's fair. Good at remembering things. Bossy. Thinks men are looking at her all the time. Wants to be a journalist and best at everything.

Sandy: Had some of that chapter too. Played part in events at Estacion del Norte. Remembers being thirsty in train and on station. Did not like the way Spanish women did their hair. Carried Morse code set under arm, so what happened to April could easily have happened to him.

April: Her chapter next. Kept saying her throat hurt.

June: Had had night with little sleep. Mouth set. Hair blowing all over the place because her headscarf was on April. Could not find hat she started journey in. Kept saying, as the train slowed down: "Well, I only hope the Naval Attaché will be here to meet us," and asking April how she felt.

Roz: Very cold and angry. Chicken was disgusting thing to have for breakfast and should have been thrown away and then nothing would have happened.

Mademoiselle: Okay so far in Spain except for being upset about picnic basket. Sighing rather. Used her Italian to speak to Spaniards which was useful.

Estacion del Norte: Cold, steamy, noisy and smelt of onions.

Dawson: High on the Rock looking out on anchored fleet in sunshine, having breakfast on his balcony, looking across bay to Algeciras which is west of La Linea.

SEVEN

THE NIGHT BEFORE, June prayed in the sleeper which she shared with April: "Please God protect us all, including Mademoiselle, and make the passage through Madrid as smooth as possible." And April coughed in the bunk above and June revised the prayer: "Please God allow us all, including Mademoiselle, an uneventful passage through Madrid and let it be the case that April's painful throat is due to irritation after sickness rather than a cold which might lead to pneumonia."

June very rarely prays specifically and keeps such pleas for times of emergency or on occasions of especial need considering it not fair to ask God too frequently for anything particular. She usually prays in general. For instance, on the night before her marriage she prayed for a happy, long and fruitful partnership rather than for good weather for the wedding. And each time she was pregnant she prayed for the health and strength of the embryonic Franklin rather than for it to be a boy or a girl and have curly hair and be good at a great many things. And usually that was enough.

She lay in bed, with a view of the elm trees the far side of the hay field coming into leaf, after giving premature birth to April. She lay as usual for about two weeks and told everyone who came in the unusually summery weather to visit her, how awfully well she felt and how amazingly strong the baby was. Alice Stephenson leant into the bassinet and said, "No, I must not lean in. These tiny babies catch germs so easily. But she *is* quite beautiful, quite beautiful."

Nanny said that this was yet another precious angel. Dawson, when he came from the Far East, said the baby looked somewhat odder than some he had been father of, but that she would, no doubt, improve. "Most people think her very beautiful," said June. "Beautiful," said Dawson. "That's all eyewash. Women go all goosey over babies. They go all haywire, moony."

April spoke a word at ten months, walked at eleven, tricycled at fifteen months and put a sentence together grammatically on the same day. Shortly after that she fell downstairs, was unconscious for five minutes, but woke up to speak another sentence, "My head hurts." At two she drew a recognisable drawing of a cow, and at three learnt first to read two new words a day, then four, then eight and then sixteen. She was on Book Two of *Reading Without Tears* by the time she was three and a half. By four she was picking out tunes on the piano, reading *Winnie the Pooh* to herself without her lips moving and could recite the whole of 'The King's Breakfast' without getting stuck. No-one boasted about April's achievements, though; they were, after all, only a few months ahead of those reached by Pru and Sandy in their time; the further down a family you are, the less there is to be wondered at in your achievement. April went on being known as brilliantly clever, but it was not talked about. At six she went to school and was immediately moved into the second form where she was continuously top.

If she were an only child, she would be much wondered at, or, if her sisters and her brother were dunces, she would be especially admired. Although she missed nearly a whole term of school after her pneumonia after Munich, she was still top at the end of term exams. Her school report reads, "Arithmetic: April has no problem with this subject. Geography: April keeps her high standard up. French: extremely good. English: excellent—remarkable vocabulary. Handwriting: exceptional." The headmistress, at prize-giving, when April took all the fourth form cups, said that Dawson and June should be exceptionally proud of April. They said of course they were proud, very proud of all their children. The headmistress said, "But this one ..."

"Yes?"

"Well, perhaps one day ..."

"Yes?"

"She might go to University ..."

Not a lot in the Franklin family was known about University. Not many people they knew went to Universities, particularly not many girls. June said to the headmistress that one day when she was not too busy she would have to find out about people going to University. She asked Mademoiselle about her University, but that didn't really count because it was in Switzerland.

People have always stared at April and April has always stared back, but politely, nicely. She has always had plenty of friends and been asked to all their parties. She falls down a lot, of course, but is not really clumsy; she just happens to trip up a lot and cut her narrow knees.

These knees between coat and dark green kneesocks jerk a bit as she stands on the platform in the cold, holding the chicken in what was Roz's carrier bag tied up with string. Her plaits are hidden under the emerald green headscarf and her face is pale, but, as has been said, April's face is always pale and goes neither blue with cold nor flushed with heat.

Her mother, holding her hand, stands taller than the Spanish people who pour past to get on to the train from which the Franklins have alighted. The engine of this train sends noisy steam up to the station roof where there are gaps in the covering glass, and the doors of the Guard's Van are thrown wide and trolleys push up the platform with the approaching crowds and against the people getting off the train, to fetch the luggage of the Franklins and other passengers arriving in Madrid.

June's voice rings out: "Now all stay close together." She takes April's hand and pushes against the moving crowd, her own width plus her shoulder bag making the gap through which April follows.

June will find a porter or Mademoiselle will find a porter and one of them will see the trolley loaded, count the pieces on to it, and then they will all go forwards to the spot where they are to meet the Naval Attaché from the British Embassy. June calls out to Mademoiselle. "We are going," she calls over passing heads, "to the office of Thomas Cook."

"Where?"

"To the office of Thomas Cook."

"Where is that?"

"It must be in the station hall."

"I see. We all go there. To Thomas Cook."

"Yes. Thomas Cook."

"I see." Mademoiselle shouts back across the heads of Roz and April and Pru and Sandy who stand between. "Yes, Thomas Cook."

Spanish railway luggage trolleys, iron wheeled and hurtling fast, cases and holdalls piled on two of these, two trolleys and four porters working on the Franklin luggage, Mademoiselle counting pieces in Italian. "Tell them to go to Thomas Cook," calls June, and Mademoiselle, in Italian, tells them where to go.

They set off under the station roof moving against the crowds, a young porter stands on the front edge of the first trolley raising his voice to scatter people in his way. Then in the wake of the first, the second trolley comes and following that, Mademoiselle, who, having no picnic basket to carry now, uses her spare right hand to hold on to Roz's left hand firmly, while from Roz's right hand, the carrier bag bounces on the uneven surface of the platform. After that come Pru and Sandy, heads down against the Spanish people milling towards the train and, lastly, June clutching April's hand, making April walk faster than it looks as if her legs can go. "That's right, all keep together." Spanish people, forced to each side by the Franklin trolleys and the Franklin progress, stare.

The first trolley noses through a wide archway into what must be the station hall, where voices echo and footsteps are on cracked and pitted tiles. The second trolley follows and the Franklins follow that. Above them as they lift their faces, there is to be seen a hole in the roof. "The rain is coming in," says April. June looks down at her to make sure the green headscarf is tied under April's chin.

The smell is of wet clothes and engine smoke, the sound is of voices, shunting engines, slamming doors. June looks up

119

to the roof and feels a spot of rain on her face and sees above the view to the sky, grey with misty vapour moving between sharp broken edges of murky glass. She clutches April's hand and goes on pulling her through the crowded hall where you brush against Spanish overcoats and find your face is close to Spanish faces.

"We'll soon be there," she says to April.

Impossible to see where you are heading with high-piled luggage trolleys and people and umbrellas. Try not to look too closely at the faces. Try not to breathe too deeply. Just keep looking, pushing, pulling April, making space for April. Because, as the luggage trolley and the others following it break through the crowds, the crowds flow together after it and block your way. And you have to elbow out another path. And April's hand, however long you hold it, never seems to warm.

April trips and tears her hand away from June's to save herself. June bends down, helps April up, rubs at the dirty knee from which a little blood is trickling. "We'll get the dettol out when we get to Thomas Cook's. It's only a graze. A graze." Refasten April's scarf and hurry on. Sometimes the tiles underfoot are slippery, sometimes they are cracked and sometimes missing. The voices echoing around sound sometimes to be English voices, but when you listen they are always Spanish.

"I can't see anyone who could be the Naval Attaché yet, but we must be nearly there." High up on the wall above the thronging Spanish heads, there is a poster of a man in red beret and with black moustache who may be Franco. Spanish voices sound like English people speaking in a dream when you are ill and lie in bed at home while people clean the house and talk on stairs and run on gravel outside the bedroom window.

She prayed last night in the Spanish sleeper, prayed generally for those at war and far from home and for those who travelled with her.

120

"The office of Thomas Cook is shut," says Mademoiselle. "And the Naval Attaché is not here to be seen."

She listened for April's cough last night and remembered the pneumonia and prayed specifically for an uneventful passage through Madrid and for no long cold waits.

"What will the Naval Attaché look like when he comes?" That's Roz's voice.

It was cold like this the winter after Munich, and they lit the night nursery fire and boiled a kettle on it. June knelt, when no-one else was in the room and prayed specifically on that occasion too.

"Why don't we get a taxi to the Embassy?" That's Pru's voice.

The wind blows rain through from the archway to the platform and through the hall and out again through the exit from the station to the city. June puts her hand on April's forehead.

"The porter says he cannot wait." That's Mademoiselle.

She knelt and prayed for April's breathing, April's temperature, April's quick recovery. And then this came. For nothing really awful ever happens, does it?

She moves herself and April into the doorway of the office. Sometimes a figure, taller than surrounding figures, dashing through the crowd might be the Naval Attaché, but it never is.

"I want to go to the lav." That's Roz.

"Well you just can't." That's Pru.

"I want us all to stay together," June says to no-one in particular.

"Why can't I go?"

You pray as fervently as you can; you cannot cross yourself as Roman Catholics do, or clutch a rosary.

The walls around the office where they wait are damp. Mademoiselle's voice reaches June: "The porters say they will have to take the trolleys or they will not get more customers."

Open your bag for money for the porters and then remember that small change at this time in Spain is stamps not

121

coins, and hand your envelope of stamps to Mademoiselle. Spanish people streaming past are putting down umbrellas and splashing raindrops outwards. You lean down with your arms round April.

Sandy has the Spanish phrase book. He turns the pages telling everyone what the Spanish is for taxi, for restaurant, for lavatory and for I do not understand.

Mademoiselle speaks fast Italian to the porters.

"For goodness sake," Pru's voice comes from somewhere. "Let's get a taxi. This is awful."

Sandy reads out the Spanish word for cold, the Spanish word for wet, the Spanish word for snow. The Spanish sentence for I need some help.

"I'll have to *go*." Roz's voice is raised.

The Spanish word for pain is *dolor*. The Spanish word for doctor is *médico*. The Spanish word for stomach and for surgery and for hospital. And Pru is telling Roz she should have gone while on the train and is a public nuisance.

And June takes out her spectacles from her shoulder bag and puts them on but they are clouded from the damp. It was cold like this but never quite as cold in fact the winter after Munich.

"I want us all to stay together."

In England you see frost on fields and rolling mist. In Spain it hits you suddenly standing in damp places.

"There must be a restaurant or a waiting room," says Pru. "At least we could wait inside."

"I'll take the little ones. Everyone else wait here."

"We'll tell the Naval Attaché when he comes."

"Tell him that's where we are."

"But first we'll be at the lav," Roz shouts.

"The lav you want will say *Senoras*," Sandy says.

You have to go through crowds again and drag a little one in either hand. You forget to take your spectacles off; they are misted still and everything is indistinct. Roz's carrier bag bumps on the ground behind her, Sir Henry Rabbit and the snake belt slip further down; you have to stop and hitch them up for her. And April's got the chicken in the parcel.

122

In the church at San Sebastian there was the red light by the altar, and there you prayed as well.

Slow progress now. They stop. Sir Henry's hitched again, the parcel under April's arm tucked firmly.

And on we go, more dragged than dragging. Your face looking towards the notice where it says *Senoras*, our faces down here bumping Spanish people in their stomachs, your hands pulling us, gripping us, us following, slipping sometimes. You're always pushing through and saying things in French to Spanish people, like *"Excusez-moi"* and *"Pardon"* so they stare and think you're French. It's hubbub, you would tell us if you were speaking to us. Pandemonium you might describe it afterwards. But we know you'll get us to the right place in the end.

You could have asked Sandy for the word for where, which way, direct me please, I cannot see; you could have had his book; he offered it. But your spectacles are misty and you have no spare hand unless you leave go of one of us.

June sees a dank doorless place reached through a passage under a sign which says *Senoras* and, inside, wet tiles smelling of the worst kind of disinfectant, the floor damp and puddled, a gutter with slithers of newspaper in it. NO FUNCIONA is written on the first six cubicles in the dim-lit passage. June takes Roz and pushes her inside the seventh door. Roz shuts the door and June stands on the outside of it; above her swings a single electric light bulb on a twisted flex.

April said that, if she came in here, she would be sick again. She would not come in, but would stay outside. She would stay exactly by this wall under the picture of this man in the red beret who was pointing in the air. Exactly there. She would not move.

June stands in the dank passage. "Hurry up, Roz." Out of the darkness at the far end, a woman in a grey apron comes with a soft-headed broom as wide as the passage itself, pushing it in front of her, its hairs bent by the pressure of the sticky damp floor-tiles. "Roz! Buck up!"

123

The woman who pushes the brush is unlike most Spaniards they have seen; has pale eyes and nearly white hair drawn back into a bun. She advances down the passage, and in front of her the broom collects a string of dirt, wet hairs and bits of paper. "Rosalind! I want you out of there." June backs along the passage as the brush approaches her and no answer comes from behind the seventh door. The brush keeps coming. June leans against the rough cement wall. "Rosalind. Come on, I tell you!" She moves her English brogues, but still they are in the brush's path; she edges, she must edge towards the exit. Without looking at the woman with the brush she calls again. "Rosalind! I'll wait outside," and turns the angle of this tunnel back into the steam and high-roofed noise of the hall outside, the black umbrellas and blown drops of rain.

Coming out, looking this way, that way and unable to see April; they should all have stayed together, stayed close together. She will say that to Dawson at La Linea; we should have stayed together definitely, Dawson; we should not have divided up; we all go together, all go up or all come down; we do not divide or separate; we always say that, don't we, Dawson, say that always? April, green scarf and brown parcel, is not to be seen under the picture of Franco on the wall outside the ladies' lavatory. Not here. Not anywhere to be seen. She simply isn't there. I don't know where she is. How could I know? And Rosalind didn't answer from the lavatory.

June's known this all along, and all along has had a feeling in her bones that it would end in tears somewhere along the line. That it would end like this, that it would happen and be bound to happen, be inevitable and come to pass that, all of a piece with April's arrival prematurely in the spring is April's departure prematurely in the winter, somewhere in Spain, somewhere in this station, somewhere here under the picture of Franco pointing in the air.

This is not happening. Of course this is not happening. This is a bad dream and you are really back in the garden, kneeling, weeding, fork in hand in cotton gloves, and the voices are from the wireless or from children playing on

124

bicycles or in the hayfield, but children's voices in the open country air are thinner and fewer than these voices. So you are not in the garden but in bed waking up from a long dream after Munich, and Dawson has gone along the landing to shave in his dressing-room, but the voices are muffled as if coming from inside gas masks. So the war has started, just started and this journey is being planned, and you could be here instead of there. And this is Roz running out of the tunnel to bump into you and shouting and dragging behind her the carrier bag with all of her and April's things inside it. Roz, who sat in the lav and did not answer and with whom one is really cross and very very angry and who, even if she roars because one shouts at her, will have at last this smack, real smack this time, Rosalind—a smack across the face cold-handed with the hand which should have been holding on to April.

Smack and grab and shake you, Rosalind, so that you drop the carrier bag with a mess of toys, books, dolls, dolls' clothes, falling on the station floor. Leave her to pick those up and start pointing and grabbing at people who pass nearest, and explain by pointing at the poster of Franco, explain to them that that was where April was standing and point to the exact spot she stood on, and point, if you wish, to the broken roof above and point to Franco again and, as the crowds stop moving past and stop and turn to stare at you, point at them and point at Rosalind and tell her that no-one should come on journeys like this. Tell her that her father has no idea what it is like being on a journey like this with children missing and children dropping things on platforms and children grumbling and children missing and children screaming and roaring when they should be helping. Tell Roz her father has no idea. And that she will be smacked again and when she says she will remember it all her life, well good! Yes, Rosalind, please remember it and let it do you good. Who cares, as Pru would say?

All Dawson would say is that people lose children and write them off. Dawson would say that there was one who disappeared in the Estacion del Norte in Madrid and was

125

never seen again. They just wrote her off of course, but June went all funny about it, went all goosey about it, went all haywire and woozy about it. June will have her picture in the paper about it, I wouldn't wonder, he would say. All those dagoes, he would say, rushing round and getting frightfully excited. June went all everything, all loud and shouting, went to everyone on the whole station about it, went to the moon about it, went on and on and on about it. They say there was a hole in the station roof and she went shaking her fist at it. They say they all thought she was complaining about Franco having bombed the station.

Roz stares at her. War certainly makes people funny, funny peculiar that is, not funny ha ha. Mothers should not hit children; she knows that very well and has often said herself that mothers never should hit children and especially not in anger. Fathers beat children, but never Rosalind. Shaken, yes, and smacked sharply on the hand, but never struck. Never hit like she is hitting. And when she's stopped hitting she grabs with iron-like grip so that one roars at her to stop; she has got out of control, as people say. Luckily the wrist-twist learnt from Sandy works and she doesn't know, as even April knows, the counter wrist-twist hold. Where is April? If April were here, she would agree that it is horrible to see one's mother with her face screwed up and shouting, looking uglier even than the woman in the lavatory with the sweeping brush. And another thing: she caused the dropping of the carrier bag, April's dolls, Sir Henry's summer uniform being scattered all over again and people with wet shoes walking on it. She screamed like she screamed the time the cows came out of the field across the border trampling on her roses. Or when the Alsatian got at Flora. She screams and grips and drags. She must be told, later, just how much she hurt and must be shown where it still hurts across the cheek which will be marked for life, perhaps, and she has loosened another tooth which will come out soon probably.

"My daughter, my daughter, *ma fille, ma fille*," she screams, getting the wrong language. Then she calls for Thomas Cook again.

There are two men, one on either side of her, in dark green uniforms and red hats. *Guardias.* They will arrest her if she goes on like that. Already one of them has a hand on her arm.

This is a time of Famine, War and Pestilence, when bombs might fall at home or where the dogs still are, a time of sighs from Mademoiselle for Switzerland and Mr Brooxbank, a time when April disappears and one's mother screams, with a strange man holding on to her.

The thing is to hang on to her, to swing as hard as you can on the other arm before the other *Guardia* takes it, make it difficult for the *Guardias*, kick them; this is war.

June stands still. Someone will come, someone who speaks both English and Spanish will arrive holding April by the hand and say, "Is this your little girl?" Someone will either come or someone will call out as they do on English stations: "Will Lady Franklin please come to the Station Master's office?" If one could hear it over the shouts of the soldiers or policemen or whatever these men in uniform are, and over the shouts and roars of Roz. The two men in uniform are badly shaven and smell of onions. Their caps are red and they have guns in leather holsters on their belts.

She ran, as a child, and as she sees her children running, through fields and along streams and went on trains and boats for treats and learnt to swim. She might have been jealous of her sister, but she learnt to walk away from her into woods and through the garden and see how trees were silhouetted against the sky and bushes and low shrubs took shape against the earth and grass, and wrote poems about all that, and learnt about herbaceous borders from her father's gardener, felt lonely as she got older and awkward in some men's company. She cried easily, like Roz cries, she was often ill like April is, she sang well like Sandy sings and sometimes laughed a lot like Pru, but never argued. She always had dogs and several cats and they sang 'As Pants the Hart for Cooling Streams' at her wedding.

127

One of her brothers died in infancy, as children did in those days, and the remaining one was the one who was shelled on barbed wire in 1918. But, before that war, he and some of his friends went to the village fortune teller who said it was very strange that their fortunes all seemed the same but would not say what was the same about them.

Many people of June's generation, many girls, never married but went on being maiden aunts which must have been awfully sad for them in spite of the fact that they did such good works and made quite interesting lives for themselves in many ways.

If you keep looking where you want to look, at countryside and lawns and children playing, you see that the world is still the same. You don't have to go to murky cities, and if you do, you stay in the nice bits, unspoilt, old-fashioned bits and enjoy the shops and clothes, and the people that you know live in nice houses like yourself and have dogs and give parties and have ponies and some problems with their children.

In the *Guardia* office somewhere on the station, the door is opened for her. Inside is steamy heat which hits you, reeking, rancid, and on a table, pulled apart and looking raw inside, the Franklin breakfast chicken, lumps of meat and bone and fat and chunks of bread. And in the corner, a pale fat man in shirtsleeves, stomach bulging over belt and breeches, with April on his knee.

But when there is a war, of course, you go wherever you have to go, like cold Madrid or to queue in passport sheds or wait on stations and, if necessary, and if asked, join the Red Cross and collect aluminium for Spitfires and raise money for the war effort. Because after the war, everything will be the same again, won't it? And children growing up as you did, awkward maybe, but to be dressed and sent to dances, parties and meet young men and be proposed to.

She was proposed to the day after she played Rosalind in *As You Like It* in the rectory garden while Dawson was visiting some friends because his ship was berthed in Portland. That was on her birthday, this proposal, which birthday

128

could not have been happier for June that June; she was married in November in lace, low waisted, with eight bridesmaids wearing organdy and carrying early Christmas roses. They are photographed, she and Dawson, in a white panelled drawing-room.

She learnt to drive a car, not fast, but erratically sometimes, never quite understanding the function of the clutch and not remembering often to have oil changed because other people saw to things like that. She learnt to switch a wireless on but could not tune it to another station. She could put a gramophone record on a turntable and wind up the machinery. She could boil a kettle and make tea, which her mother never could.

She has bad dreams of their dark blue Morris 16 in which they drove to Scotland once, careering round a hairpin bend and the footbrake suddenly not working. And when it falls headlong, containing all her children, towards a Scottish glen, it lands, not on heather or on bracken or near a salmon river, but somewhere in a town with smoking chimneys, so that the bodies of her children are smashed on paving stones or wrought-iron spikes, and there are rainbow streaks of motor oil in potholes in the street which mixes with their blood.

Which is her nightmare. And so is here and now, where April sits on the pale fat man's knee, not looking at him, but staring at the floor. Her scarf is off and laid back spread upon her shoulders, her plaits shine in the oily light, the parting in her hair as straight as ever, her face uncoloured, hands folded on her kilt. A lot of other *Guardia* here, their hats off, sitting smoking in shirtsleeves and belts, a pile of red hats and a pile of guns and a pile of meat. And April's knee still bleeding from the fall she had just after they arrived.

Hours ago that was. An hour ago, last week, last year. The heat and rancid smell soon stings your eyes. There is no air and nothing fresh in foreign places.

"I learnt my English in Nuneaton in 1925," says the Station Master. "These chocolate biscuits," he says, "are sent to me by my friends there and I keep them for distinguished visitors exclusively. Or should it be for exclusively distinguished visitors?"

June's cup of coffee clatters on her saucer: "How interesting," she says.

April smiles and drinks warm milk and eats chocolate digestive biscuits. She sits in a wide red leather chair with arms, in front of the Station Master's desk, her legs swinging a foot above the floor of his large office, the windows of which look down on the station concourse and upon the tops of the umbrellas of the crowd below. The others sit in chairs on either side of April.

"Of course we had the war quite recently," the Station Master says.

"Of course," says June.

He has a moustache and a small beard in which pieces of biscuit become caught. He has small white hands and a gold ring on one finger and explains how Spain has been so tragic a country for so long and apologises that so nearly tragic things happen to visitors to this place.

"What absolutely delicious coffee," says June. "Isn't it, Mademoiselle?"

Mademoiselle agrees. The Station Master is so interested to hear that Mademoiselle comes from Switzerland. He visited Zurich once. But Mademoiselle does not know Zurich very well. They speak German in Zurich and she comes from near Lausanne where they speak French.

Pru crosses her legs and looks out of the window, while her mother smiles at the Station Master and nods at him more often than is necessary.

"They thought there was a bomb inside your daughter's chicken, you see," the Station Master says. "So funny."

June says that she quite understands and that it really must have been terrible in the Civil War. Yes, really terrible and horrible, the Station Master says, but, as they say in England —and looking at April—all is well that end is well, it is not, isn't it?

June sits back listening to the Station Master who is, after

130

all, one of the nicest and most helpful Spaniards they have come across. These Mediterranean races have extremes of character, sometimes violent and sometimes charming. Though why a Spaniard should go to Nuneaton for a summer holiday is more than one can fathom, Nuneaton being a place not many people go to. But, in his foreign, quaint and fairly charming way, he could not well be nicer. He has even rung the Embassy to find out where the Naval Attaché is and has asked the Embassy to ring back to let the Franklins know when they will be fetched by car. And all is well: the Station Master arrived in time. The worst part was seeing April down there in that place, that room, that absolute inferno full of men who did not wash, and Roz, refusing to go inside and dragging on June's arm so that she pulled at the shoulder bag which came open spilling contents, passport, wallet, powder compact, coins scattered on the floor, and Roz kneeling on the filthy ground for the third time that day to pick things up.

The Station Master goes on talking. Pru reaches out to put her cup and saucer on the desk, sits back and recrosses her legs and sees that he is watching. He is not bad, old, but not so bad, and he is trying very hard to be nice to everyone, which should be appreciated. But one's mother is failing in appreciation, is giving up. She puts on a faint, vague cocktail party voice and nods when he talks about Nuneaton, and he, poor man, thinks she really wants to know and is very interested in him. He does not know and has no idea that she really likes people who are not like him, that she likes to be with people like Mrs Stephenson, Admiral and Mrs Burney, at the Guides, the Mothers' Union and the Women's Institute and in church. She smiles at him still, nods, smiles with her mouth but not her eyes. She's thinking not about what he says but about when the Naval Attaché will arrive.

Roz sits on Pru's right and to one side of the Station Master's desk. She could not possibly drink warm milk, nor coffee, and has had only one chocolate digestive because of being thirsty still.

131

"The little one," the Station Master said just now, "the *very* little one, does not like the milk?"

"It's a bit hot still," she said.

April, having drunk the milk, need do nothing but sit there, face rising out of the emerald scarf spread over her shoulders, smiling and looking well, and everyone is very glad that she is all right, safe and sound, and everyone looks at her from time to time to make sure she is still all right, safe and sound after her lucky escape as usual.

April keeps having lucky escapes and accidents, but is always all right in the end. She was kicked off a pony from the riding school and had concussion but no bones broken; she slid down a haystack and the hayknife went into the side of her foot but no veins or arteries were cut. Then there was the new blue bike; the first time she rode it, she was just stopping at the main road to look both ways when a van going to the farm came round the corner on the wrong side of the road and knocked her off the bike. Both the bike and April skidded sideways across the lane. April and the bicycle were brought home in the van. Her face was only grazed, but the doctor had to come and put stitches in her knee where she had fallen on a flint; she also had to have an anti-tetanus injection. The wound, when the van driver's handkerchief was removed, was open skin with jelly-like red inside, but was not actually bleeding. Blood you could see, but it was not pouring out. Stitching it up must have been very difficult, because it was not like a slice with two edges to be joined together. It was as if a piece of April's leg just above the knee was missing, and that, if someone really wanted to patch it up properly, they ought to have gone back down the lane and found the piece of flint to which must be stuck some part of April's flesh. She still has the scar, of a different colour from the surrounding skin, a bit blue in places, but it is said that it will not show when she is older and wears stockings and longer skirts.

April, who is going to be either a teacher, a Nanny or a concert pianist, has said she will marry when she is twenty and have six children, three boys and three girls, and that some of them will be twins. If having babies hurts, it will

132

not matter because April is very brave about pain, having had
so much of it during pneumonia and her many accidents.
Her mother says and her father says that when April is married they will heave a sigh of relief because of all the accidents
she has had; they seem to think that after marriage nothing
happens to people, which may be true. But if she has too
many accidents and gets more scars, she may not be proposed
to.

In the Station Master's office, April has the biggest chair
and sits with a hand on either arm of it. Sandy sits forward,
head in hands. Mademoiselle brushes biscuit crumbs from her
lapels. June has turned away from the Station Master and
looks out of the window, and Pru sits still politely.

When April gets married they will have hymn 517 which
has a verse which goes,

> When in the slippery paths of youth
> With heedless steps I ran ...

She will trip up on the way up the aisle to the altar
probably.

They were laughing just now about all the narrow escapes
April has had; they told them as funny stories to the Station
Master. Then there was silence except for the trains outside,
steaming, hissing, and voices from the station hall where
people were still walking.

Nanny has a brother who is also a Station Master of a
station near where Nanny's sister lives near Petersfield.
Nanny once took them all to see him, but hardly any trains
went through while they were there. Just one short goods
train.

The telephone rings on the Station Master's desk. "Ah, that
will be the British Embassy," says June.

Nanny's brother will be retiring soon.

"As soon as we get to the British Embassy," says June,
"will someone please wash Roz's face."

133

EIGHT

St Agatha's School, Gibraltar. January 15th, 1940.

A Day in the Christmas Holidays   *A. Franklin Form 4*

We were in Spain on the way here. We came by train to the Estacion del Norte and there I was arrested because the Spanish policemen thought that the parcel which contained a chicken, was a bomb. I was frightened. Then we went to the British Embassy. The man who took us there was the Naval Attaché. There were many houses bombed. There were not many other houses. There were people who were hungry, the Naval Attaché said. I was very sorry for them. If the policemen who arrested me ate the chicken, then they would not be hungry any more.

9/10. Excellent. *Very* nice, April.

St Agatha's School, Gibraltar. January 15th, 1940.

A Day in the Christmas Holidays   *R. Franklin Form 2*

We were in Madrid. My sister was arrested. My mother screamed. We went in a car with the Naval Attashy. Madrid was smashed to smithereans with bombs and guns. A lot of people had been shot there or died of wounds. There was not blood any more. The wounded people had probably gone to hospital. Our Suiss Mademoiselle would not look out of the window. She is a Quaker and against war.

6/10. A good try. Write out three times: Attaché. Swiss. Smithereens.

The British Embassy, Madrid. 21st December, 1939.

134

Dear Miss Bridges,

Here we are at last in this terrible war-torn city. We arrived early this morning and my sister, April, was arrested because they thought she was carrying a bomb!!!!! It was, in fact, a chicken!!!!!!!!! ...

The British Embassy, Madrid.

Dear Budgett,

Only p.c. to be bought in Madrid. Sorry it's of Barcelona. Raining here. Bought Morse code set in Paris. Love from Sandy.

P.S. Just going to have lunch.

THE BRITISH EMBASSY in Madrid faced on to a square where two main streets crossed. A flag flew from its first-floor balcony. Although many of the windows of the Embassy were broken in the Civil War, the main structure remained intact. You entered the Embassy through an arched doorway which had beside it a shield bearing the lion and the unicorn such as can be seen on British Passports and on the seal of diplomatic bags. The entrance hall was narrow but gave on to a wider hall with a marble floor and pillars, and out of this hall rose the marble staircase, rising directly away from you as you came in and leading to a huge picture half way up. Here the stairs divided and went in two directions up to the first floor of the British Embassy where there was a wide corridor leading in one direction to offices and in the other to the residence of the British Ambassador and of the Ambassador's wife. Above that were more stairs and offices and another floor.

While waiting for lunch which will be served in the dining-room of the Ambassador's residence, you could wait in a room which was called the ante-room where you could sit and read or play cards or look at photographs of the Ambassador's children or write letters or practise Spanish phrases out of Sandy's phrase book. Or you could arrange the French soldiers on bicycles on the floor in front of the coal fire. Or you could wander back along the passage to the top of the stairs and wonder (a) where Mademoiselle had gone and (b) why there was someone playing the piano a long way away downstairs.

Ten minutes ago Mademoiselle said, "I'm just going along the passage." She may have meant that she was going to the lav, but she usually says *"Je vais au lav"*, or "I'm going to *faire pipi*", if that is where she's going.

Look down the marble stairs, look up the other flight of stairs, stand at the top of the stairs and go a little way towards the offices where typewriting and telephones are heard through doors, and then go back towards the ante-room, avoiding the drawing-room where your mother is making conversation to the Ambassador's wife. listen outside the door ... and hear—

MOTHER: "It was too terrifying for words."
AMBASSADOR'S WIFE: "My dear, how awful for you."

They are probably drinking sherry.

And enter the ante-room again where on chairs and sofas sit Sandy reading his Spanish phrase book, Pru writing letters and April playing with the dolls. In another room, further away, which must be the dining-room, there is the sound of knives and forks and plates. Stand and look out of the window at the square. Some buildings opposite have just walls standing and some further along have been knocked down completely. Some of the stones and bricks which have fallen off in the war are still in the street. It is raining, it is sleeting, or it is rain turning to sleet or sleet turning to rain. Spanish people walk about because it is before siesta time and some of them wear blankets over their heads instead of scarves and coats. No-one is talking in the ante-room; it's fifteen minutes now since Mademoiselle went along the passage.

The drawing-room is a blaze of light from standard lamps and, under one of these, the Ambassador's wife sits on a silk-covered yellow sofa. June sits opposite her on a green silk chair. The carpet is gold patterned, the curtains white-

136

embroidered, and between the two women is a silver tray of sherry glasses on a table.

JUNE: "What is it, darling?"
ROZ: "Is Mademoiselle here?"
JUNE: "No darling. Are you all right, all of you?"

Close the drawing-room door and go along the corridor to the top of the stairs again and hear the distant piano. As the drawing-room door was shut, the following was said.

JUNE: "I'm afraid she's terribly temperamental."
AMBASSADOR'S WIFE: "Oh yes, aren't they? We had a French Governess for ours ... and really! I know exactly what you mean."

They are having a party tonight at the British Embassy. That was why the Naval Attaché was late coming to the station, the Ambassador's wife said earlier. This party is a Christmas party for the staff and their friends, and they are using the ballroom of the Embassy for the first time since the Civil War. When the Franklins first arrived they saw women polishing the floor in there, women dusting paintings on the wall, maids covering tables with large white tablecloths.

Mademoiselle is unlikely to be down there, but since she is not upstairs, downstairs is the place to go. The pianist must be practising for tonight, playing tunes from *Snow White and the Seven Dwarfs*. 'Some Day My Prince Will Come.' Then he changes to 'I'm Wishing.'

Metal music stands on tripod feet stand by the piano, so there will be violins and other instruments playing at the ball tonight.

One could slide on that floor, but one would have to take one's shoes off.

There are lights in the ballroom, chandeliers hanging from the ceiling. Sometimes in the Civil War, the Naval Attaché said, there was no electricity in Madrid. When they switched the chandeliers on again, many of the bulbs had broken from the shaking of the bombs. Some of the plaster from the ceiling came down also, but otherwise the ballroom was as good as new. And up on the wall there are portraits of some Kings and Queens, of Queen Victoria, Edward VII, Queen Alexandra and Queen Mary.

Mademoiselle said in the car on the way here that it was all awful in Madrid, all *affreux*, but when she looked into the ballroom on the way upstairs she said that it was not so bad perhaps, and that you could have a good dance on that floor if you had the music couldn't you?

From the ballroom there is another door, a double door of glass panels through which you can see plants growing. These doors have brass handles like all the doors in the Embassy, and open outwards. They lead, not directly to the garden but to a kind of greenhouse. Not one for growing tomatoes or chrysanthemums in pots like the one at home, but a greenhouse which has real earth between the paths and where small palm trees grow, where wooden tubs and china barrels have fat plants like lilies in them. It smells damp here like a garden after rain, and the colours of the plants are wrong because there are stained glass windows round the sides, altering the light to red and blue and gold.

Mademoiselle stands beyond some tubs and palms in an open space like a clearing in a wood. When she stands like that, arms folded and completely still, you know it's no good saying anything at all.

From the roof of this greenhouse, from the beams set between the panes of glass, hang wire baskets filled with moss and with red geraniums hanging out of them.

You could tell Mademoiselle that it might be lunchtime soon. But not make conversation. These wire baskets may have just been watered and drops fall on the tiles below or on your head as you walk under them.

Lunch will be served in the Ambassador's dining-room, but the Ambassador is away. Lunch is served round an oval table on a white tablecloth; the plates have on them the same passport shield, and likewise do the knives and forks and spoons. The table napkins are stiff to unfold and the chairs are hugely wide with velvet-covered seats, which, once you have sat down are difficult to move about on.

Present at lunch: the Ambassador's wife, the Ambassador's wife's secretary, who is a woman, all the Franklins and Mademoiselle. The Naval Attaché went to the Ritz Hotel to see if the Franklin room was ready, and the lunch he missed was roast beef, Yorkshire pudding, roast potatoes and gravy. The pudding he missed was treacle pudding.

The carpet in the dining-room is green, green and very soft like a lawn which has been mown recently. The curtains are velvet like the chair seats and, in the middle of the table, the Ambassador's wife, or perhaps her secretary, has arranged white flowers in a silver bowl.

JUNE: "Oh, I adore your Christmas roses. I suppose they grow as easily as anything in this part of the world."
AMBASSADOR'S WIFE: "Our gardener's a gem. They do make rather a gorgeous arrangement, don't you think?"

Since it is an oval table, the Ambassador's wife said it did not matter where anyone sat and that it could be a free-for-all, but it turned out that June sat next to her and the Secretary on June's right, then Pru, then Sandy, then April, Roz and Mademoiselle. So it happens that Mademoiselle is on the left of the Ambassador's wife and every now and then the Ambassador's wife speaks to her in French. But not very often.

JUNE: "What a relief it is to have real English food again!"
AMBASSADOR'S WIFE: "We are so awfully lucky with our chef."
JUNE: "Servants are going to be such a problem in England now."
AMBASSADOR'S WIFE: "Oh my dear, yes. We are frightfully spoilt, of course, with all our staff."

June wears her blue twinset and pearls and has combed her hair and put in hairpins where the curls were coming out. The Ambassador's wife wears a green twinset and pearls and a green tweed skirt to match. Her brogues are narrower than June's and more highly polished. Her stockings have diamond patterns up the side, climbing up and over each rather prominent ankle bone. The Secretary has on a white shirt, navy blue skirt and wears horn-rimmed spectacles. Her hair is fastened round her ears like earphones.

The butler moves silently between the table and the sideboard, a footman comes in sometimes. The window of the dining-room is at the far end.

JUNE: "It really is so good of you to put up with us all."

AMBASSADOR'S WIFE: "Not at all. We are delighted."

JUNE: "I expect you get all sorts of people passing through Madrid."

AMBASSADOR'S WIFE: "Not a tremendous amount on the whole. We were inundated the whole time we were in Copenhagen, though."

JUNE: "Oh, were you there before? How interesting. I love the Danes; they are such fun."

Wine for the grown-ups and water for the children, but Mademoiselle drinks water too. In French the Ambassador's wife says what a shame it is not to try the wine. Mademoiselle replies in English that she prefers the water. You can look down the table and still just see the bombed house opposite.

AMBASSADOR'S WIFE: "Oh yes. Our time in Copenhagen was tremendous fun."

JUNE: "Did you say that you were once in Buenos Aires?"

AMBASSADOR'S WIFE: "Well, we had a rather sticky time there; the South Americans can be rather a strain."

Roz, sitting with her back to the fire, unbuttoned her Shetland jersey and had it pulled over her head by

Mademoiselle. June and the Ambassador's wife both put the cardigans of their twinsets over the backs of their chairs. Pru rolled up the sleeves of her yellow jersey and Sandy sat in his grey school shirt and pink and white striped school tie. The Ambassador's wife has wavy crisp grey hair which can never need a perm. She wears only a little lipstick, evenly applied, has narrow hands, long fingers, several rings.

AMBASSADOR'S WIFE: "We had a lovely time in Rome. I adore the Italians—not Mussolini of course, but we were there a bit before his time."

JUNE: "Oh yes. I believe Italians can be very amusing. But did you know the Vernon-Hoskins there? I think he was Attaché at about that time."

AMBASSADOR'S WIFE: "Of course they were! I was such good friends with her."

JUNE: "I've known Fanny nearly all my life. We shared a governess in the war, the last war. She is one of the nicest people in the world, I always think."

AMBASSADOR'S WIFE: "I always found Vernon rather *difficile*. He's Irish, isn't he?"

JUNE: "Yes. On his mother's side."

AMBASSADOR'S WIFE: "But I adored Fanny."

JUNE: "I've always been so fond of her."

Thinly sliced roast beef which cuts easily with big sharp knives, beans and carrots in white sauce. The meat is only slightly red in the middle of each slice and there is hardly any fat on it.

AMBASSADOR'S WIFE (when most people have finished): "What lovely clean plates."

JUNE: "They've all been desperately hungry, haven't you?"

AMBASSADOR'S WIFE: "Well do everybody have some more."

But some people have not finished, namely Mademoiselle.

141

June finished first of everyone, then Sandy, then Pru and April, then Roz, who had not taken very much to start with, but Mademoiselle took very little indeed and has hardly eaten anything.

AMBASSADOR'S WIFE: *"N'aimez vous pas notre déjeuner anglais?"*
MADEMOISELLE: *"Merci, Madame, J'ai bien mangé."*
AMBASSADOR'S WIFE: "Well do everybody else have lots more."
JUNE: "How awfully interesting that you know Vernon and Fanny Hoskins."

Another footman is coming back with treacle pudding. It is darker in the street outside, the light is switched on above the centre of the table, so that you cannot see the bombed house, but only the light reflected in the window panes.

AMBASSADOR'S WIFE: "Yes, isn't it?"
JUNE: "Poor Fanny has had rather a sad life, I always think."

The butler arranges the dish of pudding on the sideboard. There are two round golden puddings, stickily infused with treacle. He moves across the window.

AMBASSADOR'S WIFE: "Of course you're bound to have heard that Fanny and Vernon's eldest is engaged at last?"
JUNE (mouth open): "Oh no! How lovely! That is good news. Do you know, I *hadn't* heard?"

The butler slices the pudding and a footman takes the first-course plates away. Looking at the window, you can see a pale watery line of what could be snow piling on the bottom of each pane. The butler puts the pudding plates in front of every place and a silver jug of cream in the middle of the table.

JUNE: "I thought Fanny and Vernon's eldest such an attractive creature when I saw her a few years ago. Do tell me who she is engaged to?"

A good half inch of treacle has soaked itself into the edge of each slice of pudding, and where the treacle has not reached, the colour of the slice is pale and buttery. You take each slice with a table spoon from the dish the butler holds and lower it carefully to your plate.

JUNE: "I do hope she's going to marry someone nice. Fanny is such a dear and does deserve a nice son-in-law."
AMBASSADOR'S WIFE: "I believe, actually, they are rather disappointed. It's not quite what they wanted for her."
JUNE: "Oh no! That's very sad."

The butler served first June and ended at the Ambassador's wife. Eight slices for eight people and another pudding on the sideboard for second helpings. Roz lowered her slice of pudding and the butler moved behind her to offer the dish to Mademoiselle.

MADEMOISELLE: "No, thank you."
AMBASSADOR'S WIFE: "Oh do! *Veuillez prendre du gâteau à la mélasse, je vous en prie.*"
MADEMOISELLE: *"Non merci, Madame."*
AMBASSADOR'S WIFE (looking at June): "Oh dear. Well never mind." (looking at Mademoiselle again): *"Est-ce qu'il y a quelque chose que vous ..."*
APRIL (looking at Roz): "She never eats treacle pudding."
ROZ (looking at April): "No she doesn't, does she?"
AMBASSADOR'S WIFE (looking at butler and reaching to take her own slice of treacle pudding): "Simply don't worry about it. We'll send for some cheese and biscuits for Mademoiselle..."
MADEMOISELLE (huskily): "Not for me, thank you."
AMBASSADOR'S WIFE: "We'll all be having cheese and biscuits later anyway." (Exchanging glances with butler and turning back to June): "Now, what were we saying?"

143

JUNE: "About Fanny Hoskins's daughter ..."
AMBASSADOR'S WIFE: "Oh yes. It's really rather a pity. I'm inclined to think ..."

The silver jug of cream is passed from hand to hand around the table, each person pouring some over their slice of pudding. Pru holds it and looks across the table.

PRU: "What's wrong with the man this girl is marrying?"
AMBASSADOR'S WIFE: "Oh nothing really *wrong*. He's fearfully handsome, Fanny says ..."
JUNE: "It's always sad, I think, if the family don't approve."
PRU: "But why don't they approve?"

At the sideboard the butler has already sliced half way round the second pudding. A door bangs somewhere in the Embassy.

AMBASSADOR'S WIFE (looking at June): "Of course, he's had an awful time, this young man, apparently. His family had to leave their home in Austria. They arrived in England with only the clothes they stood up in."
JUNE: "Oh no! How absolutely terrible!"
PRU: "He's a refugee then. What's wrong with marrying a refugee?"
JUNE: "Pru, honestly."
AMBASSADOR'S WIFE: "As a matter of fact. I think they managed to get their money out somehow by some wangle. They are still quite well off. Well, not hard up at any rate."
PRU: "Well, I think she should marry him."
JUNE: "Pru. It's hardly for you to say whether she should marry him or not."
PRU: "I suppose he's a Jew or something."
JUNE (to Pru): "Pru, honestly." (And to Ambassador's wife): "I'm afraid the young do speak their minds these days."
PRU: "I hope she marries him whatever her parents say."
JUNE (beginning to blush): "I'd rather you were quiet now, Pru. If you wouldn't mind, I'd rather you were quiet."

144

MADEMOISELLE (getting up from velvet chair): "Pru can come with me. I should like to leave the table."

JUNE (looking at everybody and not quite looking at the Ambassador's wife): "I am most awfully sorry. But Pru, you will apologise before you go."

The butler comes from the sideboard to move Pru's chair and Mademoiselle's.

JUNE: "I'd like you to apologise, Pru. Please."

PRU (still standing between chair and table): "I apologise."

JUNE: "There's no need for you to go, Mademoiselle."

MADEMOISELLE (walking behind Pru towards the door): "*Excusez-moi.*"

ROZ: "I want to go too."

JUNE: "No, Rosalind."

APRIL: "I'd like to go."

JUNE: "No-one else is going." (To Ambassador's wife): "I really am most terribly sorry."

AMBASSADOR'S WIFE: "Think nothing of it."

JUNE: "I *do* apologise."

AMBASSADOR'S WIFE: "Think nothing of it. Now who would like more treacle pudding? Really, do please think nothing of it."

Second helpings of treacle pudding were put on each plate of those who were left behind. The door closed on Pru and Mademoiselle. On the bottom of each window pane the snow or sleet piled up no more, but the half inch which had already landed there had formed a firm and frozen line.

"Think nothing of it," said the Ambassador's wife, pouring coffee in the drawing-room. "The young are, as you say, so outspoken nowadays. And the Jewish question is very ticklish, isn't it?"

"But I always think," said June, "that mixed marriages are so liable to come to grief."

145

"There is a Jewish girl at our school," said April. "She doesn't get presents at Christmas and she's bored all Saturday because it is the Sabbath."

"Oh really darling? I didn't know you had a Jewish girl at school."

"It's unfair about Christmas," April said.

"Now why don't you two run along and find the others?"

"I'd like another chocolate first," said Roz.

As they went out they heard the Ambassador's wife say that she loved younger children and was terribly sad that all hers were older now.

And they heard their mother say that it was particularly sad about the Hoskins girl because Fanny Hoskins had had a terribly sad life, hadn't she?

The Ambassador's wife said yes, hadn't Fanny Hoskins lost one of her children when it was quite young and when they lived in Singapore?

"Yes," June's voice echoes, after the drawing-room door is shut. "It died of one of those Eastern diseases, didn't it?"

"Yes, I remember now. How tragic. How really tragic for them. Poor Fanny, one thing after another."

And April and Roz ran full speed along the corridor of the British Embassy and down the stairs because as soon as they came out of the drawing-room they could hear Pru laughing in the marble hall.

You could slide on the ballroom floor if you took your shoes off and put them side by side inside the double doors. Pru sang faintly over the pianist's accompaniment and words could just be heard from the door end.

In order to get a good slide you had to start in the marble hall and take a run and then jump on to the ballroom floor. And each time you had to go further back into the hall, take the run and each time this would carry you further on your socks into the ballroom. You slid along; Queen Victoria, Queen Alexandra, Queen Mary looked out above.

The piano changed to waltz time and Roz and April took

146

a long last slide into the middle of the ballroom floor and lay on their backs, legs stretched out in front of them, looking up at the white ceiling, the clusters of grapes painted in gold leaf round the pillar tops, panting because of all that exercise and after all that food.

After that, until just before the Naval Attaché came to drive them and all their luggage to the Ritz, they went back upstairs to the ante-room. They played Consequences and for once they all played, because for once no-one did not want to.

"The Ambassador met Pru under the stairs. He said to her Mind my Bike and she said to him Your Feet Smell. The consequences were that they got lost in San Sebastian and the world said serve them right."

They stopped to wonder where Mademoiselle might be.

"Hitler met Shirley Temple on the ballroom floor. He said to her *bonjour chérie*. She said to him; you are standing on my toe. The consequences were they got married quickly and the world said they are the nicest people in the world."

They said they would find Mademoiselle when it was time to go.

"Mr Chamberlain met Mary Magdalene in Portsmouth. He said to her no smoking and she said to him *allez-vous-en*. The consequences were that they both went to live in Singapore and the world said whistle while you work."

Roz said she would go and look for her.

"Mussolini met Princess Elizabeth in Copenhagen. He said to her your lipstick is on crooked. She said to him *Parlez-moi d'amour*. The consequences were that they died of one of those eastern diseases and the world said let's all marry Jews."

The light in here is odd because of the coloured patches thrown by stained-glass window panes, squares of blue and yellow on hands and legs and diamonds of red on Mademoiselle's white shirt seen through the foliage.

"Go away please, Rozzie."

147

"We might be leaving soon."

Mademoiselle leans against a wooden roof support and up this beam there grows a climbing plant. Her shoulders can be seen, her face is turned away.

"The treacle pudding wasn't all that nice in any case."

If anyone else stood the way Mademoiselle is standing, you would think they were just standing there, arms folded. But when Mademoiselle stands this way, it is as if she is not just standing with arms folded and head still, but as if she were threatening you, as if there were weapons in her shoulders, knives pointing outwards, aimed.

"I feel a bit sick now actually."

White tiles underfoot with terra-cotta patterns on them. Roz stands at the clearing edge with fronds of fern tickling her neck above her aertex shirt.

"Jews are the chosen people, aren't they? It says so in the Bible."

The climbing plant which grows around the wooden up-right beam hides most of Mademoiselle with leaves. "And Jesus was a Jew, except that he didn't marry. At least it doesn't say he married in the Bible."

A sigh from Mademoiselle. You hear it and see, in the near darkness, that the shoulders of her white shirt move.

The climbing plant goes right up to the roof and sends its branches out in all directions. Up in the roof where the light is stronger, you can see its leaves are pale like apple-tree leaves; its flowers are pinkish white and fat and some of them are still in bud.

"Although Mummy says he was probably quite fond of Mary Magdalene."

The branches in the roof are fastened there with metal staples; they shoot out and intertwine and mix with stalks and fronds and tendrils which have reached up there from other parts of the conservatory.

"He didn't have time to get married, I suppose, because of all the miracles and parables and being in the wilderness and dying fairly young ..."

A drooping limb of the plant which starts its growth where

148

Mademoiselle is standing, hangs down by Roz's head. She pulls a leaf from it, tugs at it. The leaf is in her hand and the branch bounces up again and keeps on waving from the impact.

"But I never understand the bit where it says that he was born of David's line when he was the son of God and not the son of Joseph, because it was through Joseph that he was supposed to be related and Joseph was of David's line and, if he wasn't really Joseph's son, but God's and Mary's, then he wasn't born of David's line ... But he was a Jew in any case, so people ought ..."

This leaf is rather like an apple leaf but soft and squidgy when you squeeze it. Juice comes out of it. You smell it and it smells a bit of lemon. "In fact if Adam and Eve begat everyone and everyone is descended from the people they begat then we're all Jews really. I wouldn't mind being a Jew at all. In fact it would mean I was a chosen person and it would work out all right if we were all Jews and no-one would argue about people getting married to people who they didn't like or not getting married to people they did like, and it might be a good thing ..."

Mademoiselle has sighed again and shifted her weight from one foot to another and made the leaves rustle around her head.

"As long as it wasn't someone like their aunt or uncle's wife which it says in the prayer book you can't marry anyway..."

Mademoiselle starts walking slowly, arms still folded, towards the door into the garden where the stained-glass reds and blues and yellows hardly glow now that it is nearly dark. "What is the purpose of all this, Rozzie?"

"Just talking. Nothing special."

Mademoiselle is by the door and then moves round the clearing as if she wants to get out of the conservatory. A lion in a cage in a zoo might walk like this, and when she speaks her voice is hoarse like people's voices are when they haven't spoken for a long time.

149

"Just a few ideas, that's all," says Roz, "about the Jews and so on."

"I am not very bothered about the Jews."

"I thought ..."

"Stop thinking, then ..."

"They are the chosen people after all. It says in the Bible, Make My Chosen People Joyful."

"All right, Rozzie. That's enough. Now go. I'm coming later..."

Roz drops the lemon-scented apple leaf on to the terra cotta tiles and steps on it, treading it until, when she moves her foot, there's only a green sticky smear. "God did all sorts of things for them because they were his chosen people. He wouldn't have made the Red Sea tide go out and let them through if they weren't his chosen people. He wouldn't have shown them the way to Palestine and sent frogs and flies and boils and blains on Pharoah whenever Moses asked him to..."

"Now go away. Don't tell me stories from the Bible ..."

"They're not stories. They are true."

"I dare say so. Maybe."

"The Bible's true."

"Yes. All right then. Now, *Allez*."

"It's absolutely true."

But she walks back along the path to the door into the ballroom which is lit up now, pulling at other leaves of other shrubs in tubs and bracken fronds and sharp palm spears. "The Bible's true."

She is on the step beside the double doors, her shadow thrown on to the tiled path she walked along. "You have to say the Bible's true. If you don't believe it, then why are you a Quaker? Quakers believe the same as we do, you once said, but don't sing hymns and things about it."

"Perhaps I'm not." Mademoiselle cannot be seen but must be moving around behind the palms.

"You must be. You can't change again."

"M.Y.O.B., Roz. M.Y.O.B., and *allez*."

"I don't want to. I feel sick."

"Then go and be sick."

"All right. I will then."

"Run to Mummy."

"No."

"Then run to Nanny."

"How can I? She's in Petersfield. Near Petersfield."

"That's what you all do in the end."

"We don't."

"Go on, Roz, before I get *en colère*."

"Nanny's in Petersfield, near Petersfield and I'm in Madrid. That's silly to tell me to go to her. That's just silly and I will be sick."

"Yes and do it on the carpet of the wife of the Ambassador."

"The Bible *is* true. It says it's the word of God and God made the world and we are in the world and so it must be true."

"I don't hear you, Rozzie."

"You want us to go without you and we won't. You'd hate it if we left you here in any case."

No answer but she must be there still somewhere in the shrubs and ferns, along another path perhaps but however much you peer into the darkness, the white shirt doesn't show; there could be anything out there.

If this was not an Embassy which is important, you could scream. If the plants weren't valuable and rare as plants like these must be, you'd trample through and find your way to her. Or pretend this was a jungle like in Tarzan and the Apes and creep behind her soundlessly. You'd have a sheath knife in your snake belt and you'd take your shoes off again and do it noiselessly and in your socks. Try once more, whispering, "It's true. It's bloody true," and then push on the double doors, bursting into the ballroom where the bulbs of a single chandelier look sharp around their edges and are turning into diamond shapes, then run across the floor and into the marble hall, passing a man in uniform who nearly always stands in there, and up the stairs ...

The drawing-room is a blur of light and yellow carpet, and the face of the Ambassador's wife, surprised.

"Think nothing of it," she says again.

Nanny's armchair was green with grey patterns on it. Its linen cover fitted it exactly and all the seams were sewn in piping. If you ran your fingers all round the piping in the dark, you could follow the shape of the whole chair from its gathered skirt which touched the linoleum, up the sides, along the back rest and down along the arms and to the nursery floor again. It was not a smooth or shiny chintz, but made of linen which, where it is not rubbed by the person who sits in it, is rough; you can touch the threads and follow them, threads up and down and threads across. But where the armchair has been sat in, smoothed and worn, this texture disappears, so that you could trace and run the palm of your hand and know the shape of the person who sat here most.

Nanny usually wore dark coloured dresses to well below the knee, so well below that she might not have had knees at all, except that she had a knee to sit on. The dark coloured dresses were navy blue or green, but often for best they were a steely grey. Her hair was probably always grey, her shoes were always polished black and her spectacles were metal-rimmed.

The day Nanny left, Roz and April went in the car which drove her to the house in London where Kay and Charlotte lived. It was suggested that Roz should sit on Nanny's knee, but she chose the back seat next to April. Everyone was to be very brave and cheerful, so the least one could do was to laugh and whistle; when the others got a bit quiet, the least one could do was to go on whistling; 'Whistle While You Work', 'Heigh ho, Heigh ho', 'Some Day My Prince Will Come' and other songs. Then hymns to whistle, fast hymns like 'Onward Christian Soldiers' to be whistled slowly and slow hymns like 'There is a Green Hill Far Away' to be whistled fast, all the way to London through Petersfield, Guildford and Woking.

Just before Christmas, Pru came home from school. It was mild like the day they left England two years later, and late afternoon but just still light. Pru stayed outside, standing on the bottom rung of the field fence, feeling her pony's soft nose and in the grips of all the emotions felt by sub-teen and early teenage pony loving girls before and since. Then she went across the drive and indoors and ran upstairs to change out of her school uniform, remembering, because her mother had reminded her in the car of the change that had taken place while she had been away at school this term. That Nanny had left and that the new Swiss Mademoiselle had not arrived, and that everyone would have to be awfully busy all the holidays helping look after Roz and April.

The nursery was on the first floor with a high window under which was a window seat upon which everyone stood when they were small to look out on to the garden. The floor of the nursery was dark green linoleum scattered with white faded flowery rugs. There used to be a nursery fire, but this was now replaced with a round black coke stove which Nanny used to grumble about lighting when they had a nursery maid no longer. On one side of the coke stove was the sofa you could sit or lie on, and on the other side was the big armchair which was Nanny's chair, covered with this grey green linen chintz, which had once had on it, now hardly visible, a design of trees and bushes growing out of little hills.

Pru came upstairs to the landing two at a time and headed for her bedroom. There were always lights under the nursery door at that time of day. It was always the case that Nanny, sitting there, got up because you had just come home from school, and said how much you'd grown and how you'd soon be taller than her, which you had in fact been, several terms ago.

"Go on with you," she'd say, and, "Well I never, did you ever, see a monkey dressed in leather." And hugs were accepted from Nanny which would not have been the thing at all from anybody else.

This time there were no lights under the nursery door, but Pru pushed it open to see how the nursery would look without Nanny there. Light fell from the landing into the room, and she saw Roz; not on the sofa where children usually stretched themselves—but in Nanny's chair and probably asleep. Her head moved and lifted.

"Oh hullo, Roz."

"Hullo."

Franklins never leapt to greet each other. That was all done by Nanny. She hugged one and then the other and it may have been that that seemed to make them hug each other.

"What *are* you doing, Roz?"

"Nothing."

"Why do it in the dark, then?"

"Have you just got back from school?"

Pru switched on the light and the bulb was reflected in the bare windows where the curtains were not drawn. Roz uncurled from the chair and sat up, eyes blinking in the sudden light.

"So dear old Nanny's gone?"

"Yes."

"When's this new Swiss person coming?"

"I don't know. Soon I suppose."

"I hope she can let down hems and sew on name tapes like Nanny did."

"She probably will."

Roz stood up, still holding on to the arm of the chair, and Pru said: "I expect you're really glad about Nanny. You won't have to have your hair curled and wear those silly frocks—you look a bit more tough and grown-up already." Pru walked round the table in the middle of the nursery floor. "I mean you *were* too old for Nanny, weren't you really?"

"Yes. Definitely."

Pru went back to the doorway to go to her own room to change. "You could come and watch me change out of my uniform and then we could go down to tea." Roz did not move, and Pru said, "Well, I suppose we shall miss the old thing in a way."

"Will we?"

"Come on, Roz. Come on."

154

"No."

"What?"

"No thank you."

"Okay then, suit yourself, but don't sit down here with the light off, see?"

"No."

"No what?"

"No I won't sit down here again with the light off." Pru went away down the landing, whistling in her school uniform, to change out of it.

NINE

It wasn't anybody's fault.

The breath of six people's all-night breathing is condensed on window panes. Outside the street lights are still on. June saw their yellow glow whenever she woke up with cold; once she went to the wardrobe for her coat and covered the bed she shared with Roz. Then later she got out of bed again to fetch more coats and covered Mademoiselle and April in the other bed and Sandy and Pru on mattresses on the floor. The floor of the Ritz bedroom is uncarpeted and feels like concrete to bare feet.

It wasn't anybody's fault. The Naval Attaché had been a brick and done his best. It wasn't his fault that the night train to Seville didn't run that night and, as he pointed out, the train next day would be crowded and they had no seats. And so they had this room, the only vacant room in all Madrid.

Her gold wrist watch, engraved on the back with the date of her wedding to Dawson and with his and her initials, says half past six.

She takes her coat off the bed and puts it on over her nightdress and her money belt. She carries her pile of clothes from a bedside chair and goes across the room, stepping over Pru and Sandy on the floor, goes to the wardrobe, reaches in for the hanger which holds her coat and skirt and closes the wardrobe door again. She tiptoes between the mattresses and turns the handle of the door into the corridor, steps out and closes the door with minimum of click.

That room was so high up in the Ritz it was like a room you would give to servants in a house.

The only light in the corridor is from the bulb at the

far end which illuminates the sign which says *"Cuarto de bagno"*.

The basin and the bath are black. The floor of the bathroom is puddled where people with wet feet, but not clean feet evidently, have left their footprints.

On these wet tiles June stands in her coat and shivers. No window here, but a skylight, small and square through which you can see a covering of sleet. The puddles on the floor are icy and there is no bathmat.

Each night and every morning on a journey you think: I will not wash tonight or in the morning, because another night and another morning there may be a better bathroom and a cleaner bath or basin. This bath is black and if she put on her spectacles she would see that it is rimed with dirt from other people who have travelled through Madrid in recent weeks.

When June was a little girl she washed in china bowls filled with hot water from brass cans or from jugs brought upstairs by a maid. And in Gibraltar she will have her own blue bathroom, carpeted, a bidet, a boudoir and a ladies' maid.

But now the taps, however much you turn them on, can only let a little water drip, and that is cold.

Roz is awake and cold without her mother in the bed but everyone is still asleep. Her watch with luminous hands says seven o'clock and it is beginning to get light.

Lying on your side, you face a wall on which a cross is hung. Her mother said that in hotel rooms in England you get a Bible but in Roman Catholic countries you get a cross, so it comes to the same thing in the end. This cross stuck on the wall beside the bed is not an ordinary cross such as you get in church, but it has Jesus on it. A Holy Cross. The cross is made of wood and so is Jesus, probably. In places it is painted. His head hangs down, His eyes are closed, His lips are painted red like badly put on lipstick.

Stretch out your hands in the cold to measure it. The cross,

157

if you measure it like people measure horses, is about two hands in height, given that your hands are small though rather square, so this Jesus would be one hand high and flat against the cross and held there, flat, by nails. He is not exactly hanging but neither is he leaning. Strong nails, presumably. Or perhaps when it happened he was strapped there with a belt or rope but the man who made this crucifix forgot to put that in. They forgot to put that in the gospels too. Or perhaps there was too much blood splashing everywhere to see things properly.

It is dawning grey, as usual as it seems in Spain. Get out of bed and wipe the mist inside the window and look out. Not even enough blue in the sky to make a pair of sailor's trousers as Nanny used to say.

Returning to the crucifix, consider how the nails retained Him. Consider your own hand. There was this picture in this Red Cross book your mother had for first aid practice; it showed that the human hand inside is made of joined-together tiny bones. Now, if your palms were nailed and bashed right through and you were hanging half your weight from them, the flesh of your palms would be all torn, the small bones cracked as nails were hammered in. The same with feet. Could torn flesh and cracked bones be sure to hold a body on the cross for three whole days?

But it was not for three whole days. It was from Friday evening to Sunday morning, which is a day and a half at most. But they said three days.

It depends which gave up first, depends whether it was the flesh and bones of hand or flesh and bones of feet. If the hands went first, then Jesus would have fallen with His feet still nailed. And either His feet would have come away from the nails too as he fell, or his ankles would be broken. By Saturday evening at the latest, you would have thought.

Sandy sits wedged against the passenger side window of the big grey Ford, looking at small piles of frozen snow which have been swept into the gutters of the street. Between Sandy

158

and the driver of the Ford sits Pru, her knees pressed together to keep them away from the gear-changing lever. The back of the car is full of cases and holdalls and two of the trunks are strapped on to the rack which juts outside behind the car.

There was a thin layer of ice on the pavement in the very early morning when they came out of the Ritz to where the cars were waiting, and there were rows of icicles hanging from lamp posts as they drove through main streets. Ponds in flooded bomb-sites were frozen and had children sliding on them and some had scatterings of snow. Now they drive along a straight road south through flat country and between short winter trees along an avenue. In front of them is the other car, the black Humber. April and Roz were wrapped by the driver of that car in red blankets from the Embassy and carried across the frozen pavement.

The speedometer needle registers forty miles an hour, but the distance to Seville is in kilometres. Seville is 538 kilometres away, and since there are 1.7 kilometres to the mile, it will, at this speed consistently kept up, take nearly eight hours. Sandy works it out.

The driver who drives with leather gloves and wears a navy blue peaked cap, navy blue burberry, is the younger of the two drivers from the Embassy. He talks as he drives and answers questions. This car is a 1934 Ford V8, 3.6 litre, 70 horse power, left hand drive and is used mostly by the Naval Attaché and occasionally by the Air Attaché. The other is a 1933 Humber, 2.1 litre, 50 horse power, also left hand drive and is usually used by the Military Attaché, but occasionally by the Minister. The Ambassador has a Rolls Royce.

They come out of the suburban avenues of bare trees and take roads which are empty and have brown frozen grass verges. The Humber stays a few hundred yards ahead. June's head can be seen at one end of its back seat and Mademoiselle's head at the other. April's and Roz's heads from time to time rise into sight between. The needle on the speedometer moves round to 50 m.p.h. but the interval between the cars remains the same few hundred yards of grey flat road with stony fields on either side.

The driver tells Pru and Sandy that he would rather drive the Ford than the Humber and that he's never driven the Ambassador's Rolls Royce. He's only temporary here and is going back to England soon, to join the army probably.

The interval between the cars is so consistent that the Humber might be the engine of a train and the Ford a carriage. Between Sandy and the driver Pru uncrosses her left leg from her right one and re-crosses the right one over the left. The driver, leather gloved hands on wheel, looks ahead steadfastly at the black back of the Humber with two other trunks strapped on it. Pru looks at her silk stockings and, noticing wrinkles, hitches them between her knee and ankle, then, taking up the slack, pulls from a little way above her knee. Then she straightens the hem of her kilt, takes out the kilt-pin, adjusts the fringe edges and carefully puts the kilt-pin back.

The driver says there is a Nash, but that is driven by the Spanish chauffeur.

The sky above the two cars on this Spanish road is of unbroken grey. One cloud does not lead to another because this sky is all one grey and out of it occasionally there are flakes of snow. The driver puts his leather-gloved thumb to a switch on the dashboard; the windscreen wipers move slowly with a rhythmic buzz. They clean the flakes of snow away and then are switched off again. The driver shifts in his seat and, putting one hand in his left hand pocket, pulls out a packet of Players cigarettes: "Smoking?" he says to Pru.

"No thanks."

"Well you won't mind if I do, then?"

"No. Not at all."

Sandy tells the driver that they had an Austin 16 at home. Before that his father had a Morris. Before that a baby Austin. Pru says Sandy would not remember the baby Austin because he was too young. Sandy says that he had only said that about the Austin because he had been told about it, not because he can remember being in it. He does remember about being told about it, though.

The driver takes off his gloves to light his cigarette. The smoke crosses the car and reaches Sandy who, finding the chromium handle, winds down the window and makes an inch of air to let the smoke escape. The air outside is raw. Pru moves her legs again and her left knee knocks the gear lever. She apologises to the driver and says her legs *are* rather long.

"That's all right by me," the driver says.

Pru's hair this morning hangs rather straight on her shoulders. Sandy, because of the cold air from the inch of open window, turns up the collar of his overcoat. The driver, half way through his cigarette, pushes the peak of his cap upwards on his forehead and begins to hum.

From time to time at the side of the road there are rusty upturned lorries and deserted cars with broken windows. Also from time to time, one storey houses with shutters hanging off them. The only other traffic, and most of that seems to be heading northward towards Madrid, consists of lorries, bicycles and horse-drawn carts, but they did see one other big black car scudding past them fast.

"Looking forward to it?" the driver says.

"Looking forward to what?" Pru asks.

"Looking forward to getting there, seeing your Dad?"

"Oh yes."

The driver, as he pushed his cap back on his head, revealed blond curls springing forwards from underneath its rim. "Got a bloke there, then?"

"What?"

"Got a boy friend?"

"Not in Gibraltar. We haven't *been* there yet."

"You soon will."

"Soon will what?"

"Get a boy friend there."

In the Humber the faces of Roz and April stare back along the interval of road and both cars pass, one after the other, a signpost which says CORDOBA: 250. SEVILLA: 388.

161

"Got one at home? One to write to?"

"No."

"Go on!"

"I haven't, honestly."

"Don't pull my leg."

Pru leans forward and puts her chin in her hand and her elbow on her knee, gazing out at Roz and April waving. They make faces and put their thumbs on the sides of their heads and wriggle their fingers. Sandy, out of the right hand window, watches the uniformity of the sky. Sometimes on the horizon there is a dead tree sticking up, sharp etched and very dead.

Drivers, usually naval drivers, are to Pru and Sandy, men who lifted you up when you were small and put you on a back seat, wrapped, as April and Roz were wrapped this morning, in a rug. They might, if they were naval drivers and taking you to meet your father, have held you baby-wise and thrown you up and caught you. They might, as they delivered you to the dockyard with your Nanny or your mother to visit your father's ship, have pretended to be about to drop you over the edge into the harbour between the dockyard edge and the captain's barge. So that you screamed. Drivers called you Sonny Jim or Missy. You laughed at drivers. They were funny people. People whose hands you held like you held Nanny's hand.

This driver has blond hair and rather thick blond eyelashes, pale blue eyes. You turn sideways, if you are Pru, to establish this. No, bright blue eyes. You put one hand up to feel how your hair is hanging on your shoulders.

You have made conversation rather well, about cars and the Embassy and things he might be interested in. You even asked him, as your mother would, what part of the world he comes from.

Someone, Oenone probably, has told you how to recognise the moment when a man is interested in you, about which parts of you he looks at and the way he may show signs of nervousness like smoking cigarettes more frequently than usual. But you would have to know how many he gets

162

through normally on a journey of this length.

Sandy leans back, resting his head on the thick grey soft upholstery of the car.

"What about you, Sonny Jim?"

"What *about* me?"

"What are you going to do when you grow up?"

Sandy answers slowly: "Read the paper, I suppose, walk around, wear suits and shirts and go on aeroplanes, drive cars."

Pru says: "He thinks he's very witty."

In the Humber they have played I Spy, I Love my Love and counted towns, villages, cars and carts, donkeys and horses. They sit in a row on the back seat because the seat in front beside the driver is filled with cases. The journey has been uneventful and April has not even mentioned feeling sick. June leans back.

Really such a pleasant driver; he comes from Derby and started life working in a factory which made Rolls Royce cars. He is married and his daughters are twelve and fourteen and go to a grammar school. Really quite a good education, June believes. Derby may be a rather murky place in which to live but the driver has described the country near, the Peak District it is called. June tells the driver that she has heard that some parts of the Midlands and the North are supposed to have grand country in between the factory towns. One of Nanny's nephews had to go and live in Chesterfield.

"I live in a council house, myself," the driver says.

Roz knelt up, facing the rear window and watched the front of the grey Ford. Then she sat down again and leant against Mademoiselle. She kicked the red Embassy rug on to the floor soon after they left the Ritz because it was leg-restricting and rather like a shawl.

Mademoiselle stares out of the window. She is huddled in her overcoat of air-force blue. This morning, when everyone was arguing about who was going in which car, she was the the only person who said she didn't mind which one she went

163

in. She simply got into the Humber and sat in one corner with her hands in the pockets of her coat.

The driver was a prisoner of the Germans in the last war. He also worked on a farm near Frankfurt where there were Polish girls also working.

"I feel very sorry for the Poles," says June.

"What were the Germans like on the farm?" says Roz, leaning forward.

"Nice enough folk," the driver says.

"But they took you prisoner."

"Not the same Germans as I worked with on the farm. You can't bear a grudge to folk you work with."

"Is that why you aren't fighting in this war?" Roz is gripped by June's hand stretched across April, and is kicked by April. "I only wondered." Roz leans back again. She stares out of the window. "It's quite brave driving cars."

April kicks again.

"Council houses are very nice these days, I believe," says June.

The driver's council house in Derby is only five years old and has metal windows. His wife does not like the windows because she says they will rust, but the driver thinks they are all right, modern, but all right. But he's been away from home for six months on the trot so he could not say if they have rusted yet. His wife does war work, making shells or bits of shells; she doesn't know which bits or where they fit into the shell. He left the Rolls Royce factory and took a driving job abroad because he got restless living in Derby all the time. He thinks it is something to do with having been a prisoner of war.

The shape of his head and the way his grey hair shows round the base of his navy blue cap somehow reminds June of Hudson, the gardener at home. Rather a dull drive though, she thinks. This part of Spain is very dull indeed with broken cars and army trucks left by the roadside, and the houses in the villages and towns unpainted and uncared for. And no gardens. "It's such a dull and dreary part of Spain," says June.

164

Mademoiselle puts up the collar of her coat. Some of the time she has her eyes shut. She played I Spy and I Love my Love and then went quiet again. But at least you can sit beside her now and not feel daggers coming at you. By Roz's watch it's noon. Sometimes Mademoiselle changes when it gets light and is different in the morning. At other times it happens in the evening when the lights go on. Seville is south of here and it is difficult to tell what time it gets dark there in winter.

The driver of the Ford having lit one cigarette and put it out, soon lit another. Sandy opened his window wider. The road changed from flat to sloping, gears were changed more frequently. You began to see out of the front window of the Ford a deeper view of countryside ahead and below. The sky was lighter. The air still biting cold on nose and forehead, still damp and raw, low bushes on the roadside still hard and stiff, broken down cars still had white frost patches, rime still on blades of grass. Nothing moving anywhere except the cars, no animals in fields and only people wrapped in scarves or blankets, in the towns and villages. Not many towns or villages either. Sandy watched an opening in the sky among the clouds ahead. The car nosed down another slope with rocks on either side. And up again.

But there must be a wind somewhere because between the rocks, tall weeds like ragwort move. Something stirs their heads and stalks, something which is not only from the passing of the cars.

Pru leans back on the seat she shares with Sandy and lets her hair hang over the back of it. She shakes her head and stretches her legs as far as they will go under the Ford's walnut dashboard. She's told the driver about school and School Certificate which she would have taken if she had stayed at school, but which she is really much too grown up to bother with these days. School, of course, is boring, terribly, because of being only girls. A lot of people run

165

away, and Pru herself would have run away if she had had to stay there any longer.

A steep and downward road and the opening in the sky was nearly just above. The Ford, in low gear, took the gradient. Far down, a bend. Beyond, a plain, and on that plain a sunny patch, lit lime green, and a curve of what might be a river flashed like silver for a moment and went dull again.

They sit up forward, holding on to the dashboard, peering out. A gorge below them to their right; Pru leans over Sandy to look out. A hair-pin bend; another gorge below them to their left; Pru leans across the driver to look down. Then a more gradual slope with grass on either side, and there is the Humber drawn into the verge because it must be time to stop for lunch.

Here is the Embassy picnic-basket lunch; ham sandwiches, hard boiled eggs, apples, biscuits, coffee in thermoses and fizzy lemonade. It was not warm enough to eat outside so they ate in the cars, parked one behind the other on the road edge, rocks and grass below them on the south side of the road and rocks and grass above them to the north.

They walked, at June's instruction, away from the cars to stretch their legs. Sandy climbed northwards to the tallest rock outcrop. There was a platform of rock on which you could stand and see the plain spread out below you. Sandy climbed down, but jumped the last few feet and landed on the squelching Spanish grass.

There was a wind, coming up the hillside and felt around the ears. It was a bearable, sniffable wind which came around you, and you could take your hands out of your pockets and turn down the collar of your coat again at last and lift your chin.

The only hills beyond this hill are foothills. The mountains are behind. Sandy looked at April's atlas before they left Madrid and saw that, on the physical map, the country was shaded green south of the Sierra Morena. Madrid was on a light brown land; south of Madrid was dark brown land; south of that more light brown, then pale green, then darker green. Once they get to the darker green, they will be as good as there. Down to Cordova and then Seville along the valley of the Guadalquivir river.

The Ford goes first this time. The driver drives without his gloves. His hands are large with small blond hairs on the lower joints of all his fingers. The cuffs of his white shirt show below his dark blue jacket. Beside him Pru and Sandy sit without their coats on and with the window open wide.

"Like going on a holiday, isn't it?" the driver says.

"A bit," says Pru.

She has told him about leaving school and about how she will have to do lessons on the Rock, but that when she is old enough she will go back to England to do war work if the war's still on. And she's told him that she will probably be a journalist in the end, that she won't marry for years and years and that when she does she will go on being a journalist and may not bother with having children.

Sandy sticks his head out of the window and wonders if the driver wants to know all that.

They go through avenues of poplars on flat roads, and these trees, although dead for winter, have single yellow leaves clinging to occasional branches. Where the sun is low it flickers through between the poplar trunks.

On the other hand, Pru might be an actress, she tells the driver, because she took the part of Cecily in *The Importance of Being Ernest* when they did the play at school. It was an *ingénue* part unfortunately, but quite a big one. The driver says he does not know that play but he likes films so why doesn't she try to be a film star.

"That might follow, I suppose," says Pru, "from being on the stage."

A bridge across a river and a town where streets are empty because it is siesta time. Above the hum of the Ford engine a church bell sounds, deeper than any English church bells Sandy has ever heard.

She might equally well choose factory work, says Pru, and although she won't marry for years and years, she will have

167

plenty of men friends because you have to look around before you choose the absolutely right person.

"Lucky if you get a Mr Right," the driver says.

When she does marry it won't be in a church but in a Registry Office, nor will it be in a white dress, nor will her choice be influenced by her parents. But she will have a party afterwards for special friends and most of her relations.

The driver edges the speed up to sixty miles an hour because the road is straighter here and wider. He checks in the mirror above his head to see if the Humber is in sight. He seems to be listening to Pru still and says she is a proper caution.

She will marry absolutely anyone of any creed or any colour, but first she will have a frightfully good time. The driver nods, pushes his cap further back on his head and scratches his neck above his white shirt collar.

Her mother had a terrible time when young, a very boring life and never went away to work or even went to school. It was lucky for her that she met Pru's father. It might have been much worse. Her mother is old-fashioned in lots of ways but she lets Pru choose her own clothes now and wear lipstick often. Really whenever she wants to wear it. Really she can do exactly as she likes.

Sandy watched the pink sun disappear beyond some distant hills and then be seen again. Where people, Spanish people, were walking behind ploughs in fields, he watched the earth turn under metal blades. Because of the war there could be bullets turned up in these fields. The driver says he will be driving back this way tomorrow because the Franklins will have naval cars sent from Gibraltar for the last lap of the journey.

TEN

JUNE HAS A room all to herself, with a marble wash-stand and a brass jug of hot water which the chambermaid has brought. The room has shutters folded back outside which, when she first came into the room, she reached out over the street and drew towards her, shut, because the sun was out. It shone then through the slats of the shutters in sharp parallels. But now it's nearly dark and the shutters are thrown open.

The bed is far back in the cavernous room, but, when you lie here in the fading light, you can see across the street, arched windows, iron verandahs, red geraniums on window sills. June takes off her jacket and her brogues and lies down on the high carved bed hearing Spanish spoken in the street outside and English in the passage of the small hotel. She lies on the white linen counterpane, one arm flat beside her and one hand touching the string of pearls; she looks up at the whitish ceiling. The walls of the room are pale and on the dark brown floorboards there are rush mats. It is six o'clock and nearly dark; at home it would be the little ones' bedtime, but their voices echo from the next room and their footsteps run on wooden corridors.

When she first came into the room it was siesta time and the street outside below the window was empty. Now, at six o'clock, a car engine passes, a horn hoots, cart wheels rumble and horses' hooves are heard. She was thirty-eight last June and her hair shows small bits of grey when she studies it under a strong light and with her spectacles on.

The air became warmer through the open window of the Humber as they drove towards Seville. April was never sick, nor felt it. April has no cold, sore throat and one way and another it could be, cross your fingers and touch wood, that

169

everything is going to be all right. The driver was a brick, the Naval Attaché was a brick, the Station Master was a brick and so was the King's Messenger in many ways. Perhaps June has been a brick too. It has been quite an achievement after all. Quite an ordeal into the bargain, she will tell Dawson when she meets him at La Linea in the afternoon tomorrow.

She lies on the high white bed and, with any luck, can stay there until dinner time; no-one need come in. Pru's voice is strident as she calls to April and Roz in the next room where all three are sleeping.

They saw the bell tower of the Cathedral from miles away; they watched it coming nearer for the last half hour. Then they were in Seville on cobbled streets with palm trees in the evening sun.

June: thirty-eight, ten stone, hair fanning out on pillows, dozing until dinner time, dinner in yet another hotel dining-room with Mademoiselle and the children and all the decisions about who will eat what and who won't eat at all. Really it would be rather nice to stay here, going to bed at the children's usual bedtime. For two pins June would stay here, have a snooze, miss dinner.

Last year she had been married for fifteen years and Dawson gave her the naval rating's reward for fifteen years' good conduct, three V-shaped stripes which the blue jacket wears on his upper sleeve, one stripe for every well-behaved five years. June's good conduct stripes are framed in mahogany, her name is underneath engraved on brass, and they hang beside the double bed at home. If ever she deserved the stripes, she must deserve them now.

At the Admiral's house high up on the Rock there will be red bougainvillea and purple bougainvillea hanging in swathes above the front door, and arum lilies in the garden, which grow like weeds. Last time she saw the Admiral's house she was six months married and five months pregnant, Pru kicking on her stomach wall as she lay in the guest wing under a mosquito net, four months before Pru burst out into fifteen years of not particularly good conduct. People say one child

170

in a family has to be difficult. June closes her eyes and hopes not to hear Pru's high voice until dinner time.

But it echoes in the corridor: "All right, you two! Shut up! I'm going. No, I don't know where Sandy is, or Mademoiselle. Or Mummy, come to that. So shut up and stay there."

June opens her eyes in the half-light and cannot but help hoping Pru will go downstairs and not come in here. Children are difficult or not difficult, strong or delicate, have straight or curly hair, fat legs or thin legs, blue eyes, green eyes, brown eyes. They are born musical or unmusical and arrive out of pain and effort into their frilled bassinets where people lean in and say who they are like and what they will grow up to be. Mothers lie back on pillows, monthly nurses and nannies bustle in the room and mothers sleep with clouds of glory in the birthplace of the bedroom.

Roz goes along the corridor and upstairs to the room which is Mademoiselle's, but the door is locked and when she knocks there's no reply, so she goes downstairs again right to the ground floor of the hotel, across the foyer and towards the glass doors which lead, it seems, into a garden.

When June was a little girl they used to bring you bread and warm milk in bed and read a story to you. Flames flickered from night nursery fires.

Sandy was going to get the Morse code set to work. He said that when he'd fixed it, Roz could tap at one end, he the other.

They call this a garden, but there is no grass, only paving and dry earth with spiky bushes growing in it. And there are buildings round it on every side, parts of the hotel with lights in windows. This is more of a yard than a garden, this is. But there is a pond in the middle, round and with a smooth cemented parapet. Not a deep pond. If you kneel on the ground and lean up and over the parapet you can just touch the water and, if you lean a few inches further, you can touch the bottom of the pond where there are slimy weeds, but, as far as can be seen, no goldfish.

June breathes evenly, her mouth a little open. Somewhere

171

on this floor is another bedroom, Sandy's Morse code set begins to bleep. The bleeps are buzzes, short for dots and long for dashes.

Having knelt and looked down into the water, Roz then stands up and steps on to the parapet and balances there, placing one foot in front of the other, arms stuck out stiff like the wings of an aeroplane, and circles slowly in her kilt, her aertex shirt and snake belt. There is not much else to be seen in this ungardenish garden, but there is plenty to be smelt. The dry leaves of the spiky bushes, if you pick a leaf and crumble it, smell sweet like fruit drops or like women's scent, expensive like the scent Aunt Kay wears or like a dress shop or a hairdresser's. In some parts of this square courtyard with rounded arches all around it, it smells like Hudson's greenhouse at home when the tomatoes are nearly ripe.

Funny to be in a so-called garden in the dark. Summer darkness comes when you are in bed and this is winter darkness, but still warm. Midwinter night. They did *Midsummer Night's Dream* at school, but in broad daylight. April was the fairy Mustardseed in yellow organdy, skirt sticking out all round and with a plaster on her knee, pirouetting on the school lawn with the plaster hanging off. Roz could have been Cobweb or Moth but said she would be either Puck, the Changeling Boy, or nothing. She balances on the parapet and circles it again. She was nothing in the play.

Eyes get accustomed to the dark. They give raw carrots to Air Force pilots to make them see. Stand by the pond and now see everything in the garden, each tree in its tub along the terrace, the flowers on a creeper hanging down over the arched walk in one corner. A flash of white where someone walks along behind the arches. And in the doorway from the foyer, Pru, in her new yellow cotton frock from Selfridges, blinking at the darkness.

Roz kneels by the pond and dips her hand in it again and stays there while Pru comes out of the door and turns along the cloisters and is seen passing behind the creeper in the corner, walking towards whoever was standing there just now.

It seems to be the driver of the Ford who's standing near a window but not quite in its light. They say that the pupil of your eye enlarges after time spent in the dark, so that you can see people who have only just come into it and they cannot see you. But it might be wise to crawl forward from the pond edge to the shelter of the nearest spiky bush. From here the wide-eyed, dark-accustomed viewer can see clearly into the cloisters and not be seen. Can see the white shirt-front of the driver and the yellow dress of Pru and see two cigarettes lit and even smell the smoke drifting in this direction and mixing with the bush which smells of pepper.

There are whispers and there is Pru's cough because she hardly ever smokes. Then she throws the cigarette away and it glows red on the cloister floor in front of the lit window. The driver moves into the light to tread on it with his polished shoe and moves back against the wall again.

When they start kissing it is really very like the films, Pru's hand on the back of his neck and her head tilted sideways so that their mouths can match. And when they part again they breathe rather heavily because of the time they were kissing when they could not breathe. Then they kiss again. The luminous second hand of Roz's watch ticks round thirty seconds for this kiss, and the third kiss lasts forty, while their bodies move against each other. They say that for kisses of this kind you have to have your mouth open and you let the other person's tongue come right inside which sounds disgusting and unlikely. But, if it is the case, then when they part there could be a sucking sound.

This may be what Mademoiselle did with Mr Brooxbank on their Sunday picnics. Perhaps Mademoiselle did not like it and therefore gave up Mr Brooxbank and said she could not marry him. But the driver is rather nicer-looking than Mr Brooxbank, especially his hair is nicer, shining blond when every now and then he steps back into the window light. And Pru has made it lift up from the back of his neck when he was kissing her. Or was she kissing him? Or was it that they kissed each other? The taller person must do the kissing because they have to bend down deliberately to do it.

173

And usually the man is taller. Unless he found a stool or wooden box to stand the woman on. Which might be more fair.

After the kissing, and while Pru's arms are still up round the driver's shoulders, they seem to be rubbing their cheeks together rather like birds do their beaks, or like cats rubbing their faces against your hand.

Once Pru laughs, but, not having heard the words of the whispered conversation, it is difficult to say what she is laughing at.

It gets very boring after a time in this pretended garden. The paving is hard under your knees. The smell of pepper any minute might make you sneeze. There are insects on this bush and in your hair and, looking towards the double glass door into the hotel hall, Mademoiselle can be seen coming down the stairs with her knitting bag.

Pru will see you move, though, and Pru will say, "You were spying," and you will say, "I never spy. I just happened to be in the garden. I left just after you came out. I did not see anything in the garden. Anything wrong. It's not wrong to kiss someone, is it? I didn't see anything in the garden and spying is only when you look at something you're not supposed to look at."

Mademoiselle is knitting white ankle socks again. Last time she knitted they were on the train to Paris and she has not knitted since.

"Hello, Mademoiselle. I can see you are knitting again."

"Hello, Rozzie. What have you been doing?"

"I have been in the garden, Mademoiselle. Not for long though."

"What is it like in the garden, Rozzie?"

"Oh. Very boring. A very boring garden. Not a garden at all, really."

"What is happening in the garden?"

"Nothing."

"Nothing?"

174

"Oh yes. The insects are biting. I think they are mosquitoes. And the bushes are smelling and there are no goldfish in the pond."

"I see."

"Un jardin tout à fait ennuyant, n'est-ce pas?"

"Where is Pru?"

"I haven't the faintest ... I don't know."

"I thought she was in the garden too."

"No. She's not anywhere out there. I didn't see her anyway. I think I'll go upstairs now and see what April's doing."

June opens her eyes. The room is dark but the door into the corridor is open and there is enough light to see that Mademoiselle is standing near the bed.

"What is it, Mademoiselle? Is it time to eat already?"

Mademoiselle's eyes and hair are too dark to see—the pale of her cheeks and forehead and the bright white turned-back collar of her blouse are all that June can see.

"I was having such a lovely snooze. What is it? Where are all the children?"

The corridor outside seems empty, no footsteps there or on the stairs, no voices from the next room and no cars, carts or horses from the street outside. Sandy's Morse code bleeps no more. June half closes her eyes. "Has something happened to the children? Is something wrong?"

The silhouette of Mademoiselle shrugs its shoulders and turns away.

"Have they done something? Have they said something? It's very naughty of them if they have."

When it got really dark and cooler in the bedroom, June took off her skirt but kept on her cardigan and got, not properly into bed, but under the counterpane. She sits up holding the counterpane under her chin, face turned to Mademoiselle.

"They haven't done or said anything, Lady Franklin."

"Well that's all right then." June leans back again against the pillows.

"People do not have to do anything or say anything to make things wrong."

"I don't know what you mean."

"No. So I will say no more. I should not have disturbed you."

June leans back, head on pillow, face towards the window.

"I feel in my bones that something has happened. Has there been a message from Sir Dawson? Has something happened about the car he's sending? One of the cars? Is there some trouble about the rooms? Where is everyone? Where is Pru, April, Sandy, Roz? *Où sont les enfants, Mademoiselle?* Is some of the luggage missing?"

Foreigners are strange: strange and temperamental; you learn that as you go along. Even Americans who speak the same language are different, June has learned.

"Are you feeling ill, perhaps, a bit?"

"They do not need me."

"Oh Mademoiselle, of *course* they do. We all need you. We are all so fond of you. I don't know what we'd do without you. And all through this journey you have been a brick, an absolute brick."

"Like the King's Messenger and the Station Master and the Naval Attaché at the Embassy?"

"I don't understand you. The children are so fond of you. Is it that you want to leave? That would be awfully sad, and I honestly don't see how you can just now. It's so complicated being in Spain, and even when we get to Gibraltar, I don't really see ... I know that Roz is very babyish and stubborn sometimes..."

"I have said that I will stay ..."

"But you might have changed your mind. Sir Dawson and I would always understand ..."

"I have said I will stay until Roz is sent away to school ..."

"Well that's all right then."

"*Then* I will go. You will not need to send me; I will go."

"The war is bound to be over then."

"And see the world ..."

"Oh I see! The world. Oh yes. How lovely. Travelling ..."

176

I think everyone should travel. Not like this, but when you're unattached ... that's one of the advantages of ... well it would be lovely ..."

Mademoiselle seems to be going away. Arms folded, head down, she walks towards the door, her rubber soles squeaking on the boards. It has often been like this with Mademoiselle, half giving in her notice and not explaining why. June sits up in the bed again and wraps her arms around her knees. The thing about having a Swiss person was that you felt they were less volatile than the French or the Italians.

"Oh, Mademoiselle ..."

She turns. "Yes, Lady Franklin?"

"Er ... is your room all right?"

"Oh very nice. Not bad."

"That was a nice man, the driver, wasn't he?"

"Oh. Very nice."

"And Mademoiselle?"

"Yes," standing just inside the door, the light behind her, face unseen in shadow.

"It will be lovely in Gibraltar."

June is leaning back again in bed and staring at the ceiling. There was a photograph, a snapshot, Dawson sent, himself in uniform, white summer uniform, sitting on a canvas seat suspended from a metal frame, a swinging garden seat with trees above it on a sunlit terrace.

"And ... Mademoiselle?"

"Yes, Lady Franklin."

"I wonder. Do you think? I wonder, do you think you could be awfully kind and ask them in the dining-room if they could send my supper up here on a tray, just boiled egg and bread and butter and perhaps a cup of tea? They seem so nice at this hotel and might do meals like that. That's what I'd absolutely love."

She turns on her side under the counterpane towards the slatted shutters. Once she saw the nursery wing at the Admiral's house. The day nursery was huge and had a door on to a paved verandah, where there were white-painted wooden tables and chairs, tables for playing on or having

nursery tea. Two of the Gibraltar Apes, orang outangs from
the Rock, a mother and a baby, were sitting on the balustrade
against the bright blue sky. Mademoiselle can't help but cheer
up when she sees the nursery wing, with the view, the Apes.
You could not ask for any better childhood place.

She told them in the car today about all that. They know
about the ponies and the dogs already there and that they
might get a puppy if they stayed there long enough, but only
if they stayed there long enough. You couldn't take a puppy
back to England she explained, because of quarantine; six
months in kennels for a puppy would be cruel.

They were driving through Cordova: "Dogs have to wear
muzzles in Gibraltar," June explained.

"How cruel," said April.

June said: "It's because of rabies. Not because they want
to hurt the dogs."

They were coming near Seville and through the archway
of the Roman wall: "There aren't a lot of dogs in Spain,"
said Roz.

"The happiest dogs are English dogs," said Mademoiselle,
who had not spoken for some time.

"Oh, absolutely, Mademoiselle," said June.

"You keep your dogs until they die."

"Of course we do."

"But people you can send away."

"We sometimes have our dogs put down," said Roz.

"You put your horses out to grass."

"We sometimes have them shot," said April.

The palm trees in the squares of Seville threw sharp shadows
on the Humber as it passed.

"Who do we send away, then, Mademoiselle?" asked
June.

"Children to school and gardeners and cooks and maids
and Nannies. You keep your dogs and horses until they die,
but people like that you send away."

June snoozes on her bed in her hotel room in the evening

and wishes that she had said to Mademoiselle that usually such people quite want to go in any case.

Next door Pru lies on her bed, smiling. No. Roz looks at her. Smirking, is what Pru is doing. She wasn't in the garden very long. April reads. Sandy put Roz's end of the Morse code set down by the door but the bleeps have not come through yet. Silence. Someone coming down from the floor above, soft soles on stairs and squeaking soles on boards outside this room. Squeaking soles going on down the lower flight of stairs. Roz gets off the bed and follows.

In the foyer the swing door is still swinging. Outside in the street people are walking slowly under streetlights. None of these slow walkers will be Mademoiselle who was moving fast when she was heard to go downstairs. Her white blouse collar is the thing to look for and there is a white something on the far side of the street where there are tall buildings and an archway. The white patch is moving and the movement is the walk of Mademoiselle, the way she walked across the Place de la Concorde in Paris or walked around the house at home to check the blackout.

It is colder than expected; the Shetland jersey might have been the thing to wear. The thing to do is to keep moving, staying on this side of the street where there are lit shop windows and where people seem to be walking in the opposite direction, not hurrying but wandering. You have to keep as close against the wall as possible without scraping it. Across the road, Mademoiselle also moves against the crowd. It's difficult to be sure which white patch is her because a lot of women who walk in Spanish towns at night wear white. But luckily no Spanish women who are out tonight wear white socks. Mademoiselle crosses the road towards this side and the street comes to an end.

People are looking at you so you don't look at them. Keep going. There is no law against someone of seven who is English being on a street like this. Anyone can walk anywhere as long as there is no notice which says Private or

Trespassers Will Be Prosecuted. No war is going on in Spain any more, no enemies for people to look out for, not even any bombs fell on Seville to speak of, so the driver of the Humber said today.

Roz goes round the corner: Mademoiselle turned right.

Sometimes at home she walks and walks and sometimes she just bicycles and bicycles, not saying where she is going before she goes, or where she has been when she comes back.

Turn right into a darker street where not so many Spanish people walk. You can just see from this distance that Mademoiselle has her shoulder bag but not her suitcase. But she can fit a lot into that shoulder bag. Once she said she could travel for weeks with only that, as long as she had money, toothbrush and clean knickers. Once she went on a walking holiday, just after her year at University, in the Alps with just a little knapsack.

Here is a piece of the city wall they drove through earlier: it goes all round Seville the driver said. This street seems to run beside that wall, the top of which is in the dark above the streetlights.

Mademoiselle stops at a street corner and looks up at the name of it, but then goes on. Perhaps she is heading for the railway station.

Turn right again and leave the city wall. Also leave most of the people walking and leave the buses and the cars. This is a narrow street with cobbles. Coming into it was like entering a tunnel and, if you look up for just a second, you see how close the upper windows are together. Not many streetlights here. Lamp posts are far apart, but under each one as she passes, you see her shirt and socks and then she goes into a dark patch until the next light, never turning round.

In this street it is as though it rained a little while ago. A cobbled street with cobbles which are slippery. A funny smell, not quite of onions, not peppery like the spiky bush, but funny. Not many people here, but some are standing outside houses, talking to each other. They stared at Mademoiselle and now they stare at Roz. Walk on, ignore the stares. A lot of Spanish women seem to have no teeth. Only walk

180

faster when there is a bend in the street in case she turns and sees you. Keep the space between you like the space was kept between the Ford and Humber. But wish you had your sandals which have rubber soles.

Once she said that, walking in the Alps alone, she used to sing, but she isn't singing now.

A crossroads here, but Mademoiselle goes straight over it and into an even narrower street with even fewer lights, and only she is walking here and not many windows have lights in them, and no-one stands outside their doors. This street is one which goes on longer than any street you've ever known.

Once she said you had to sing quietly in the Alps because loud singing might bring down an avalanche. But she isn't singing even quietly now.

There were voices before in the street with shops and, in the street beside the wall, there were people moving near you. Even in the first narrow street they looked at you and said things to each other outside their doors. But here no-one is standing, talking, moving.

Cobbles underfoot pressing through leather soles, socks slipping down round ankles, but no time to stop and pull them up and who would dare?

Sometimes—traffic noises, engines, hooters a long way away. Otherwise no sound between the high houses which seem empty. Their doors are shut, locked probably, and their windows have iron bars in front of them. Not even, like before, a smell of Spanish food. But narrow alleyways, openings which lead away to darkness. It may be that the people who live here are in the alleyways.

You could call out. This street must have an end. If it does not have an end, you could call out to Mademoiselle.

She would have to turn round and come back if you called.

She would have to. But she's going faster.

The thing to do is not to look into the blank black entrances of alleyways. And not to look at windows with iron bars in front of them. And not to look behind, but try to catch her up.

Once she said it's better to go alone. If you can go around the world alone, then you are not always waiting for someone else.

The people in this street may be in the alleyways or they may be standing in dark rooms behind barred windows, looking out, moving curtains, watching you. The curve of the street curves on and Mademoiselle goes faster still. Anyone could be in the alleyways or behind the windows. Anyone— Germans, *Guardia* or even ghosts.

Mademoiselle has never seen a ghost, she says. No-one in the family at all has ever seen a ghost. Sandy says that no-one he knows has ever seen a ghost. You don't believe in ghosts.

They might be in the alleyways or they might be in the houses. Nanny said that, if you saw a ghost, you could get rid of it by holding up a holy cross and telling it to go away. Otherwise she didn't have time for holy crosses.

If you don't believe in ghosts, you'll never see them, Roz's mother said.

But even if you had a holy cross and it was a Spanish ghost, you could not tell it ...

Sandy says that no-one has ever taken a photograph of a ghost. That proves it. No-one's proved that they are there. But have they proved they're not?

The Spanish for "Come here" is *venga*.

But the Spanish for "Go Away" is not remembered. You could try French of course.

Keep following. Cobbles slide away under leather soles. Ghosts: they say that just before you see a ghost you feel extremely cold. And often when you should be warm. But here it is cold and damp but you are hot from hurrying.

Don't look there. What did you see then? Nothing. Don't stop. Hurry up. Go on. Buck up. *Depêche, depêche.* Where is she? Further round the bend. She should be there. She must be there. She has to be. Last seen here. Just here under this streetlight. The streetlight's here and she was here. She *was* here. Call. You'll have to call.

You see, if I stop walking I might hear other footsteps, so I keep on walking even when I can't see her ahead of me.

182

I have to keep on walking, nearly running, because of what might be behind me.

You see, if I stop and shout, whatever is behind the bars and in the alleyways, would hear me too.

You see, I have to go on. I really think I have to go on. Even past the lamp post she was passing when last seen. Even when there's nothing up ahead except more street, more alleys and more windows.

My mouth is open ready to shout out. I think the sound will come. I'm running now, and if I go on trying to call out, the sound will come eventually. It will echo when it comes, like running footsteps echo. I do not know the Spanish word for help.

The sound that comes is slow to start, a sort of rumble, getting louder. Low to start with but then rising and filling every corner of the street. The loudest noise possible, louder than the fog horn on the Channel steamer, however near you stood to it, louder than the largest piece of brass the Royal Marines have ever blown. This noise comes from above first and then from all around. Hands over ears, then fingers stuffed in ears, but you can still feel it through your feet. You would have thought the houses all around would fall down because of it.

You have to stop, hands over ears. You cannot hear the noise you make with shouting.

It was like this waiting for her to come to the Gare d'Austerlitz with the luggage, like this standing at the edge of the conservatory in the Embassy, like this when she went out on Sundays and came home by bicycle.

Reverberating and still resounding but now recognisable as a clock which struck and is still striking, each note taking a full second to sound each hour.

So she wasn't going to the railway station; she was going to the cathedral. At seven o'clock exactly by the luminous hands of Roz's watch and by Seville Cathedral.

She is there across the road as it happens. A light shines over this entrance to the cathedral. She is up some steps. She must have had a white headscarf in her shoulder bag. She has it on because you must put something on your head to go in somewhere Roman Catholic. She might be going in or she might be turning this way. If you stand under this lamp on this corner of that long dark street, she might still see you. Wave. With both hands, wave. It's rather a wide space to cross to get to the cathedral door; there are tramlines and trams on them occasionally, but people are walking in that space.

"*Arrête*, Rozzie, *Arrête. Tais-toi.*"

"*Mais, mes pieds ...*"

"Serve you right. You shouldn't have followed me."

"We're not going the right way. We didn't come this way."

"*Dépêche-toi. Dépêchons.*"

"I suppose you're going to be a Roman Catholic."

"Tosh!"

"I bet you are. Do they have them in Switzerland, Roman Catholics?"

"Pish and tosh I tell you. *Allons.*"

Across the Plaza del Triunto, the Plaza de la Alianza and the Calle de la Acazaba because the *Guardia* outside the cathedral told them that was the way to go back to their hotel. Mademoiselle still wears the white silk headscarf and pulls Roz along. They walk against the stream of people going towards the Plazas out of the side streets. Mademoiselle is singing now. You cannot hear the words, but the tune's familiar.

"Guess what I was going to see?"

"A cross, an altar, a tomb, a holy painting?"

"A tomb, but whose?"

"A saint's?"

"He wasn't that."

"A he?"

"*C'est ça. Un homme. Quel homme?*"

Someone selling flowers under a palm tree on the corner of a square. Shop windows bright. Mademoiselle still sings: "A clue for you, Rozzie. They all laughed at him."

"When he said the world was round?"

They didn't actually go into the cathedral, but they will tomorrow early in the morning. This evening they walked about outside it, looking up at huge windows and arches and Mademoiselle said it was certainly the biggest cathedral in Spain, if not in Europe, if not in the world.

Roz said: "I thought St Paul's was."

"You would. How typical."

They sang across a square and when they came to a café with tables in the open air they wove their way between them as you go between posts in a bending race on ponies at gymkhanas. This time they sang, 'We joined the Navy to see the sea'.

"If you are typically good, then it isn't a bad thing to be typical," said Roz.

"And what did we see, we saw the sea. We should all go to America, I think. Are you cold? Let's run."

"And if you are typically bad ..."

"I said, let's run ..."

June sat up in bed with the supper tray on her knee and tapped the top of the soft-boiled egg with a teaspoon. Then she separated the segment at the top, lifted it and laid it on the side of the plate beside the egg-cup and took her first mouthful of bread and butter. Then she poured some tea out of the teapot and added just a little milk. Mademoiselle had done wonders with the head waiter.

Then she lay back and heard them all going downstairs for dinner.

Mademoiselle seemed quite cheerful again when she brought the tray and said that she and Roz had had a nice walk round Seville. No, they did not go into the cathedral, but passed nearby it. It was shut anyway. June said it seemed that Spanish churches often shut at night, but they would all go round it in the morning if there was time.

The snooze and the doze had done June so much good. She finished the egg and bread and butter, drank two more cups of tea and put the tray back on the marble-topped bed-side table.

After dinner the children came in to say goodnight to her, the maid to take the tray away and June was ready to settle down for the night, hearing doors close along the corridor and children's voices fading. But Sandy's Morse code set began to bleep again.

Nanny used to say, "Goodnight, sleep tight, don't let the fleas bite." These Spanish sheets are crisp and cool. "Up the wooden stairs to Bedfordshire." "Sleep tight, wake bright," Nanny used to say as often as she said that things would end in tears.

Nanny herself never cried, except the day she left, and then she said: "It's just a speck of dust in my eye from all that packing." They gave her sherry in the drawing-room.

June turns on her side towards the open window and pulls the counterpane up over her right shoulder. There are Spanish voices in the street below, but she will sleep.

Nanny liked sherry, just a glass, and always had one on her birthday. You never knew how old Nanny was. As old as her tongue and a little bit older than her teeth. Good health, Nanny, Dawson used to say.

Opposite the good conduct stripes in the bedroom where June sleeps at home are the four studio photographs of four babies, which were taken in Portsmouth, where June used to drive, with Nanny in the back seat with the baby to be photographed on her knee. The earliest photograph, of Pru, is in brown and white, but the later ones of Sandy, April, Roz are grey and black and white as most photographs are these days. The babies lay on their stomachs, Nanny arranged a shawl for them to lie on the photographer's table because you never knew what sort of baby might have lain there earlier. The same photographer took all four photographs in the years between 1925 and 1933, and they were all taken at the same age, six months old. To the untutored eye, the babies look the same. April, of course, looks the smallest, Roz looks the biggest and fattest and Pru is still smiling the most and is often said still to smile the most. Sandy looks solemn and is still said to be a solemn person.

Four times you gave birth and four times you took us to the photographers. In between and at other times you took snapshots of us in the garden, crawling, staggering with push-carts on fat legs, or, in April's case, on thin ones. Sometimes we wear sunsuits and sometimes coats and leggings and some-times we hold puppies or kittens or stand in gumboots and woolly hats. Sometimes there is, in the corner of the snapshot, a woman's skirt which will be Nanny's, as she was standing near. Not that there are not a few pictures including Nanny, sitting in the garden holding one of us, with her straw hat on, Nanny wearing the hat, and whichever it was of us, a bonnet. Or a sun hat if it was Sandy.

You look at all the snapshots which you keep in the bed-room on the chest of drawers under the studio portraits and on the opposite wall from the good conduct stripes and say: "You see, darling, even then you were fat or thin or smiling or sad or clever or silly or rude or difficult or stubborn or determined or musical or unmusical or tiresome or sweet or possible or impossible."

Once, it is said, Sandy drew a moustache on the picture of Pru lying on the photographer's table on the shawl Nanny put there, and it is said that he got beaten for it in beating days. You don't like photographs changed like that.

You say you always know what a baby is going to grow up like, but how can that be possible? People can change like photographs can have moustaches added to them. Sup-posing one of us got terribly scarred by bombs or was attacked by a lion in the London zoo if you ever take us there again? Or we might go from Gibraltar across to Africa and meet a lion there. Most people who have been mauled by lions are dead because of the poison in the claws, but Sandy's friend Budgett's uncle was mauled and is still alive. But very changed of course, with scars.

Mademoiselle said you can change from being typically one thing to typically another. Or, she said, you can change or be changed by knowing people, seeing things and never be the same again; it sometimes is the case, she says. She said that coming back from the cathedral.

It will be the case, it could be the case that we might lose our hair or have smallpox; we all have smallpox vaccination marks on our legs, which were not there, the vaccination marks, when we were born. Nanny once said if people cry a lot, their mouths get turned down at the edge for ever.

June, while sleeping in the Spanish linen sheets, would still believe that clouds of glory must come into it somewhere.

Sandy saw Gibraltar first. Right in the distance from a plateau, he saw it sticking up out of the Atlantic. It looked, he said, exactly like the postcards of it. It looked small at first and mostly white because the sun was lighting up the water catchments which are lined with limestone and are near the top. But you could see patches of green as well, red roofs and smoke.

The naval driver said they should be able to see the coast of Africa too. But there was a mist beyond Gibraltar which meant that the wind called the Levant might be coming in their direction.

They came down off the plateau and there was a very flat white road. It was somewhere here that one of the naval cars slowed down and stopped.

The driver of the other car saw them stop and stopped in front of them. The two drivers lifted the bonnet of that car and looked inside. They said it was the petrol pump.

On either side of this flat white road there were rows of little bushes which could have been olive trees, but possibly young vines. There was nothing else to see at all.

"I just can't believe that anything can go wrong now," said June, throwing off her tweed jacket, then her cardigan, and feeling the sun on her arms and back.

The petrol pump could not be mended, both the drivers said. So the other car, which was all right, would go on to Gibraltar with a message. It went, with Mademoiselle and all the luggage and she arrived at Gibraltar first of all.

While they waited there was nothing but white road, low fields of vine or olives on dry earth. The grass on the verge was dry as well and it was hot. To the right there was a distant mist and to the left was also hazy, but the road straight south, down which they looked expectantly was clear like spring as far as you could see.

It came into sight about two hours after they had broken down, a speck on the horizon throwing up white dust but with the chromium on the bumper shining. And as it got nearer you could see in the front seat of the car, the white of a naval officer's cap and a touch of gold which would have been the braid and crown, and all those rows of medals.

Sandy would say you could not see medals at that distance.

They turned their heads as they sat on the bright red rug they'd kept by mistake and which belonged to the British Embassy in Madrid. The white dust from the dead straight road rose in a cloud to the south, and through the cloud came the royal blue car and, on its bonnet, the white St George's cross, the silk white ensign Admiral's flag with no dots on it, blowing in the breeze ...

Sandy would say that, if a car was coming straight towards you, the flag would be blowing backwards and no part of it would be visible, except for the metal staff off which it flies.

The car approached, whether or not the flag was visibly displaying the insignia of the Admiral and, as it came up out of the sun, we stood up and shielded our eyes with our hands as we were wont to do. It was as if we were having our photographs taken by someone with a vast camera coming from the south. Then we all stood and waited, the driver at attention and saluting. And he got out of the car and then we saw the white of the cap, the medals, the epaulettes, the face you had almost forgotten, the arms held out ... and the next day, which must have been Christmas Day, we went to the cathedral and there we sang a hymn of thanksgiving for our safe arrival. There was a huge white square in front of the cathedral and we were driven down from the Admiral's house in the royal blue car with the flag flapping. Rows of

189

blue jackets lined the entrance, presenting arms; they wore flat white hats and good conduct stripes and we sang 'Eternal Father Strong to Save Whose Arm Hath Bound The Restless Wave'.

It was in fact dark when they came to the Rock; the moonlight steeped in silentness, the bay being white with silent light and it was not Christmas Eve, but the day before that, the 23rd. So the day they went to the cathedral was Sunday and not Christmas Day. And the hymn they sang was not for their safe arrival but a customary end to every service which included members from naval establishments, and was sung at the end of the service, after the blessing, the congregation kneeling. Only the last verse was sung in fact, which goes 'Oh Trinity of Love and Power, Our Brethren's Shield in Danger's Hour'.

If you look through your fingers as you kneel there are choir boys in blue robes and white frilled collars, kneeling also and looking across the chancel at each other as they sing.

The cross on the altar is ordinary brass like most crosses on most altars in most churches or cathedrals.

Out of the window this morning there was a smell of heat and flowers. You had to lift the mosquito net to get out of bed and look down on to the bay which was full of dark grey warships. Then you could walk out on to the verandah you had been told about so often and look up to the top of the Rock where the Apes were supposed to come from.

They stood after the service in the porch of the cathedral with their eyes shielded from the sun. They were hot in the same winter clothes they travelled in because their summer things had not been unpacked.